MONSTER

MONSTER
unearthed

BY BOB W. CANNADY

PALMETTO
P U B L I S H I N G
Charleston, SC
www.PalmettoPublishing.com

Copyright © 2024 by Bob W. Cannady

All rights reserved

No portion of this book may be reproduced, stored in a retrieval system, or transmitted in any form by any means–electronic, mechanical, photocopy, recording, or other–except for brief quotations in printed reviews, without prior permission of the author.

Hardcover ISBN: 979-8-8229-5120-4
Paperback ISBN: 979-8-8229-5121-1

Heroes obey the Geneva Convention, but a monster has no rules. They are out of the scope of rules and laws. When you want to take out a monster, don't send in the military; send in the monster. They have no affiliation with anything—no country, no agency, nothing. They are in fact no one. If the need is to combat evil, send in evil.

TABLE OF CONTENTS

Chapter 1	Introduction	1
Chapter 2	Picking the Monster	6
Chapter 3	Test Two: Skill Test	30
Chapter 4	Test 3A Final: Navigations/Survival (Isolation Mountains)	56
Chapter 5	Test 3B Final: Navigations/Survival (Isolation Desert)	78
Chapter 6	Test 3c Final: Navigations/Survival (Isolation Jungle)	111
Chapter 7	Interrogation and Explanations: Next Phase	142
Chapter 8	Training to Become the Monster	150
Chapter 9	Meeting One of Me	172
Chapter 10	Observation	178
Chapter 11	Talk Time	181
Chapter 12	Mission Time	187
Chapter 13	Distraction	194
Chapter 14	Jungle Killing and Destroying	202
Chapter 15	Jungle	209
Chapter 16	Brutality: Last Mission	223
Chapter 17	Living with Yourself	237

Chapter 1

INTRODUCTION

I started off in a small town in Montana. I had a mother and a half brother. My brother would leave every time he was upset with Mom and go to his dad's. I, on the other hand, did not have a father; he was killed before I was born. I had nowhere to go but to stay put.

My mother did the best (I guess) she could with only an eighth-grade education. She dealt cards and worked in various bars and restaurants, trying to keep us fed. However, there was a downside to all of this. She would meet men in bars or truckers at restaurants and bring them home. Then, depending on my age, I would either have to leave or stay and listen to what surely was sex. I hated this! I would have to see them come and go just so Mom could get extra money for gambling, drinking, and food. Not a healthy life for any child to grow in.

I could almost deal with that because that became normal life for me. The part I struggled with was the constant abuse from boyfriends and husbands. They would end up beating her up and then turn on me and finish the job. All my younger life seemed to be full of fighting, abuse, and drinking.

Needless to say, the kids in school were ruthless toward me. I received beatings from all kinds of kids. Mostly older ones. The whole town knew my mother, and I took a lot of the wrath from the kids. Mom also would buy me second-hand clothes, which got me made fun of by other kids. They would tell me all the time, "That used to be mine." Ha-ha. Really made me feel lower than dirt. But what do you do? My mom didn't have lots of money, so that is what I got to wear.

There was one way out during my school years. I started participating in sports. I took track, wrestling, and football. In the summertime I worked cows and moved irrigation pipe. During those four years of high school, I became bigger, meaner, and stronger. I no longer had to take the crap from other kids. I pushed myself to be the best that I could be.

However, I did make one error in my school years. I remember one week before state champion wrestling when we were not allowed to drink. I went to pick up my girlfriend at a party. Everyone was trying to get me to have a drink; I didn't want to at all. But just to appease everyone, I took a sip—that was all. Yes, I was in the wrong. Well, the next day my probation officer said, "I heard you were at the party; did you drink?" Of course, I lied and said no. However, my conscience got the best of me. So, I did admit to the sip. He told my coach and got me kicked off the wrestling team. I was mentally crushed to death. I had so much hate in me at that time. I lost my chance to go to college and ended up a loser. I got into fights and got assault charges against me and was on a one-way ticket to prison.

My brother asked me to come and live with him in Fallon, Nevada, to finish school there. He was in the navy. I moved down to get out of town and try and start a new life. During this time, I figured I had no chance for college anymore and had no money, so I joined the marines.

During my time in the service, I realized something important. I went back to my hometown and found that probation officer and told him he'd taught me a valuable lesson. He asked, "What is it?"

I told him, "Never to tell the truth. That is what you taught me. I was always under the impression that if you told the truth, they would be more lenient on you. That isn't so true. It cost me everything." (My fault I took the sip.)

So life went on. I spent eight years in the marines as a reconnaissance sniper and three years in the army as a Special Forces.

After my tours were done, I wrote my first book, *Through the Scope: Memories of a Sniper*. I had some issues that I needed to express so I could move on with life.

Writing the book was the best thing I ever did. It helped me cope with the loss of my friends and also helped me find God. I had never been a God-fearing person, but after that I found him and tried to walk the line going forward.

After I was out of the military, for a short time I became a police officer like most ex-marines. That is all we know: anger, fighting, and death. So, I joined up and fit right in with them. However, as time moved on, I found myself becoming more and more depressed about some of my military experience. Not sure if it was PTSD or me—I just felt like I screwed up in life and judgment.

I decided to kill myself once and for all. I went up on a mountain and had it all planned out and asked God to forgive me for what I was about to do. At that time, the poem "Footprints" popped into my head. I asked the Lord if he was trying to tell me something; I didn't know if he was carrying me at that time and was telling me to get up and do something different. What that could be I had no idea at that time. Then college popped up again. I picked up my gun and quit my job and moved home.

I started college and worked various jobs and received my education. I was still struggling in life, so I asked one of my psychology professors, "What should I do?" I didn't want to tell anyone or go to counseling, so he told me to write it down. So, after ten years, I finished my life in the military and put it into a book. It helped me tremendously.

After college I went back into the army to try and give life one more chance to take me out. I figured that I had cheated life; all my friends had died except me. So, for three more years, I volunteered for everything. Nothing happened, so I guess I was forgiven, and it was time to move on.

I had two beautiful boys during that time, and life was good. So I moved on to the next job. I found work in the oil field. I thought this would be a great-paying job to support my family. Little did I know, but people were watching me for the next few years. When I say people, I mean the government. In fact. the oil field was the perfect environment for what was coming. I could move around and no one would expect anything different. I sometimes wonder if they had the oil field find me and seek me out. Maybe this is what truly happened. I guess I will never know that part.

What people don't know in this world is there are government agencies that seek out people like me. People who have great tendencies to become violent don't care about life, and yet they function in society. I was the perfect candidate for what was coming. I thought of it like being a serial killer. They function in everyday life, but yet a switch goes off and they turn into something unrecognizable. Family, work—nothing matters—only the job set forth. They saw this in me, and they used it to suck me into their society. Like I mentioned, people have no idea what is out there and who they might be dealing with. But pray to God you don't run across them; they are dangerous and deadly.

This is my story of how I went from being a family man with children to a monster. As I stated, a monster has no boundaries and does not work under the Geneva Conventions. Monsters operate under no laws; they do as they are told, and they do the task for money, but most of all because they enjoy that part of life. Adrenaline!

Chapter 2

PICKING THE MONSTER

Picking the monster!

How do they go about picking someone to do all their dirty work? I didn't even know this kind of person existed. Basically, they pick a person who is very aggressive, has no conscience, and has killed before. They like highly trained individuals from the US military; this is their prime focus. It's like they observe you and your life from the moment you enter and until you get out. Of course, I don't have any idea if that is true; I am just guessing.

I was very highly trained in the marines. I showed no remorse for anything except the loss of my comrades, but other than that I didn't care about anyone or anything. Maybe this was due to my childhood, which I am sure they knew about too.

During my time in the army, I do remember seeing guys in suits appearing around and asking questions. Didn't pay much mind to them at all. I guess I should have.

MONSTER

The question in my mind that I will never know the answer to is this: Why did they wait two years after I got out and had children until they came and found me? I was doing a normal job and raising a family. Of course, at this time my wife had left me, and I was vulnerable, I guess. They asked me to serve the country one more time.

Of course, I had no idea what they were referring to. They asked me several questions about life and how I was coping with it. I do remember telling them I missed the structure of military life and that I wished I never got out. They also asked if I missed the action. Of course, who wouldn't?

They said I could keep my job and they would talk to my bosses, and I would move up in the ranks very fast and pay would move up even faster—but only if I was a successful candidate.

I remember asking them, "What does that mean?"

They told me, "First you will live like a normal person and have other jobs set forth." Also, I would have to do as I was told without question. They asked me if that was possible.

I immediately said, "No problem."

They also told me that there would be some very strenuous tasks set before me, and I had to complete them without flaw and again, no questions about why or what I was doing. I would be told, and that was it. I was held in silence from that day forward, and no one would know who I was. Needless to say, I was a little concerned about what I was getting myself into. But what the hell—I needed some excitement in my life.

That night I lay in my bed in WY and wondered what I was doing. Was this the right thing to do? My family was gone, I was all alone, and I had nothing in my life worth anything. I just wanted to live and die.

Within the next few months, I didn't hear anything. I was not sure what was going on. Why didn't they come back? Then I got ordered to go to Africa. Wow, OK. This would be a rotation job: thirty-five days on and thirty-five days off. Were they doing this, or what was happening? I really had no idea about anything.

For about three months, I went to Africa and did my normal job. I guess I was learning the job to become more proficient and building my résumé. No idea if they were ever coming back, so I just proceeded to be normal and move on.

When I flew back to the US after one month, I was met at the airport by a man. He introduced himself and said I needed to come with him. My first test of the screening was going to start soon.

This was like, "Wow—I am really going to do this crazy shit for the government." I actually thought they had forgotten me.

I can't explain my excitement at going back to work and doing something that I loved. I had made up my mind that no matter what they asked of me, I was going to do just that. It didn't matter about life, nothing. I just wanted to be needed. Again, I think this feeling came from my childhood experience. No matter what, I was going to do anything they asked.

Test 1: The Room

I was asked to get into an SUV with dark windows and put on a mask that completely obscured my vision. They put a needle in my arm, and out I went. I woke up sometime later, with no idea how much later. I was dressed in garments like hospital clothes but not really. I felt like I was underground. There were no windows and really no people. It was dark and cold. Really freaked me out at this point. I was fed some kind of loaf for food and some water and sat by myself for an hour or so. I guess I needed to get my head on straight after being drugged out. Again, I had no idea where I was and how long I was out.

One man came into the room after a short time and told me the rules. I was not allowed to ever mention anything about what I was doing. "Like I don't even know what the hell I'm doing anyways," I said. He told me this was part of the training. I was not allowed to mention anything about the government, working for them—nothing. The only things I could talk about were very small details of my life: nothing major, nothing about my military career, nothing.

He made it very clear that I was nothing and would be nothing from this time forward, and I could never trust anyone or anything. He told me bluntly, "You are no one; you have no number, no name; you do not even exist. You have no affiliation with anything. Do you understand?" I told him I did. He repeated that I would be watched every minute and judged on my actions. Anytime I did not follow the rules, there would be grave actions taken against me.

I thought, What the hell does that even mean? Are they going to kill me if I screw up? Of course, I was not even sure where I was or what the hell was even going on. But OK, I was ready for anything. I knew the main rule: follow orders and don't even deviate from them. Do as I am asked, and it will be all right. I guess.

He left, and I sat there for another hour or so.

Then a man came into my room and motioned to me to come with him. He didn't even say anything to me. He was a big burly man who looked like some kind of monster with scar on his face and mean-looking eyes. Whoever this guy was, he was not nice. I could see by his so-called military clothes that he was a no-nonsense type of guy. I'm not really sure if he was some kind of security or what, but I can say this: he was one guy that bothered the hell out of me.

I got up from my table and walked to the door. He motioned for me to go ahead of him. I could see he was carrying a Glock 21 45 cal. on his hip and a kukri knife on the other. Of course, he had about four mags also on his belt and a radio. I really felt uncomfortable with this guy.

I proceeded to ask him where I was going and where I was at. Again, silence; he didn't even acknowledge I had said anything. Very strange.

The layout of the so-called corridor that I was walking down was also very nerve racking. Picture a long tunnel made of cement that smelled wet and mildewed. The lights were there but not exactly bright. There appeared to be rooms with doors on both sides as I walked down, not a lot of them but enough to make you wonder what was beside them. The corridor itself was eerie and made me feel very uncomfortable. The corridor also was extremely long and had many different paths you could take. I could have very easily gotten lost, one way or another.

So I did what any good marine would do: I just went in front of the man and waited for him to point in the direction I was supposed to go. I found it very ironic that he never once talked to me or made any indication at all. He was a very difficult to man to try and understand. One thing for certain is that he was not one you would want to tangle with.

I remember telling him that I really had to go to the bathroom; I was about to crap my pants. He looked very annoyed at me and pointed into a room. I walked in and saw a toilet, a shower, and a non-made-up bed. Of course, no door on the toilet. He just stood there. I thought, This is even weirder, but I had to go. I sat down on the toilet and crapped my brains out while he stood there looking at me, pissed off. Shit, I have to go—give me a break, I thought.

After I was done, I got up and went back to the door and out in the corridor. I was thinking all this time, Bet you shit, too, you big fuck! I was really getting annoyed by this time. I guess it was all the silence and unknowing maybe. Regardless, I was half–drugged up and tired of his shit by now. I just wanted to get where we were getting to and get on with it. Little did I know what was ahead of me.

After a while I was escorted into a room with another man, who was dressed like me and looked to be quite a bit younger. I could see cameras everywhere and glass mirrors. I assumed that was the camera and people behind it. There were two chairs in the room and a small table in the middle.

The kid started in talking, asking what the hell was going on. I replied I had no idea. Of course, they had told me that I was held in secret and that I could not say anything about anything. So I just played along like I didn't know anything either.

He went about telling me that he was in college and had been kidnapped, leaving his girlfriend's house in a black van. He asked me what happened to me. I replied, "A similar circumstance." He did ask me what happened to me. I told him, "Pretty much the same thing." I reiterated that I didn't know anything either.

He asked if we were some kind of government experiment or something. I told him, "I have no idea if we are kidnapped by government or some serial killer. I really have no idea what is happening." He was freaking out. I told him to settle down and tell me about himself and relax. "I am sure eventually we will know what is going on," I said, "but until then, let's not panic and remain somewhat calm."

Then he started in about his loving family that would miss him so much and that he was afraid to die. I reassured him that we were not going to die and that we would both make it out. He then asked, "How can you be so calm about all this?"

I said, "I'm not calm about all this. I'm very nervous as well, but as of now there is nothing we can do about anything, so let's see what is happening to us first."

He kept asking if we are an experiment of some kind for the government.

"Again, I don't know. Why do you keep asking?" I asked.

He said he just thought all of this looked like government, and he said he'd seen movies and this was what it looked like. I tried to reason with the kid and tried to relax him. But it was not very much use.

He asked me about my life. I basically told him the good points and that I worked in the oil field and I had two sons that I loved very much. I didn't go into depth too much but enough to keep the boring room out of focus. He kept on about his college and girlfriend and how they were going to have kids and get married after he graduated. He genuinely sounded like a good kid.

I asked him what he was doing in college, and he told me it was government. "What does that mean?" I asked. He told me that he wanted to expose "the secret society of the politicians" and tell the people. That was a big red flag if nothing else was ever said.

I now knew why he was here, I guessed. But still he was just like any other kid who wanted to get to Big Brother and find out the secrets. They stood no chance of ever finding out what goes on behind closed doors. Whatever, I thought.

The more we chatted, the more I really liked that boy. I could sense the bond growing between us. I guess I felt like he was a private and I was his sergeant. I needed to look after this kid. Even though I kinda knew something but not really. I could not understand what two different people like us were doing in the same room in this godforsaken place.

I had no idea why he was in here; to be honest, he didn't fit any profile like me or military. Just an ordinary kid going to college. I have to say I was really confused as to why he was in here. However, there was some reason why they put him down here with me, and that was about all I knew at this time. Regardless, we had to make the best of it and hold on for what was next.

After a few hours of chatting with my new buddy (we were bonding because of the circumstances we were in), we were fed the same crap I had a few hours ago. Wrapped-up loaf and a plastic bottle of water. Really tasted like crap.

As the hours went on, I had to use the bathroom, and so did he. But unfortunately, no matter how many times we requested to go, no one came to the room. I do remember asking the mirror if we could use the bathroom, and nothing. So we both peed in the corner. That smelled like piss! We both laughed and seemed to be making the best out of a shitty situation.

We talked about various things again, and both had some laughs and sad moments. Missing families and such. I really felt close to the kid. I actually talked about seeing him again when we get out of whatever this was. Again, I was confused about why he was here.

Then the most dreadful thing in my life came. The last hour or so, I found out.

The Last Hour
The guy came back in the room and told the boy he had to sit in the chair. The boy sat down crying and asking, "What is going on?" The man reassured him that everything would be fine and he would be let lose in the hour.

The man handcuffed the boy to the chair, rearranged the desk in front of me, and put my chair behind it. He showed me a red countdown clock and said, "When that reaches zero, you have to use this gun and put one bullet in his chest." Then he asked, "Do you understand?"

I nodded.

I was so confused. What the hell is this? I thought. I can't shoot this kid! I almost went to the mirror to go tell them to fuck off. I had no idea what this test was about or why I had to shoot some poor kid who was tied up and helpless.

The boy was screaming, "Please don't kill me—please don't!" He was losing his mind and begging me.

I was so confused in this act of cowardness that I just didn't know what I was going to do. I knew I had to do it, but why him?

After sitting there not listening to the kid, I had to make up my mind whether to do this cowardly act or not. I can tell you that this was not an easy decision to make. However, if I wanted this life, it had to be done, and for some reason they wanted him killed. I figured it wasn't up to me to decide what to do, but just do it. If I chose not to, I would be out, and he was surely dead anyway. So I made the tough decision to take his life.

The next thing that popped into my mind was, Do I do as they ask or show more and walk over and just break his neck to show my commitment? Either way the boy would be dead, and I would now be part of the team. Or so I thought! In actuality I really didn't know how many more of these so-called tests there would be and what they entailed. All I knew was they asked me to do something, so I would try and do what they asked and more. I had to show my worth and strive to outdo the ones before me. I had to be the overachiever.

In the military they always asked for volunteers, and I always raised my hand. I volunteered for everything. This turned out to be in my favor, because after a while they were sick of those that didn't volunteer and would pick them for the worst of the tasks. So volunteering for everything actually was the best thing for me. I was always picked for the best schools and promoted above all my peers. The ones who never volunteered were never promoted or asked to attend specialty schools—only those that strived to be better than the rest were. I guess you could say this is one of the reasons I was chosen by them to be a part of their team.

The clock was counting down second by second. If I didn't do what they asked even after I'd agreed to, what then? Would they kill me too? Second by second, I kept watching the clock. I have to say that the last hour seemed to be longer than any other hour I had in my life. I kept thinking about what this kid was saying and wondering,

Why him? Again, I was going to fulfill what I needed to do. He was going to die. By this time I figured I would go beyond and show them my commitment and just break his neck to show no remorse and show them I was ready to commit to anything they asked me to do.

The boy was begging for his life time and time again. Time was running out, I glanced at the clock, and fifteen minutes had passed while I had been in my own head wondering about all of this. I really don't remember much of what he was saying because I was too deep in my own thoughts. I would really like to know what part he'd played in getting himself here? Was he here because of his schooling? Was he here because of politics? Was he here because of something his family had done? Or was he just some random kid off the street for me to kill?

If you really think about it, people are just sheep, and the wolves prey on them daily. They don't care if they are sweet or mean; they just kill them without a second thought. People are just sheep; they have no idea that government or people in there don't really care about them. We all like to think they are looking out for us like a sheepdog protecting us from the evil, but maybe *they* are the evil. We are nothing else but a small piece of the puzzle. We, you, don't matter at all to them. I hope you all realize this. There may be one or two that do, but not much more than that. They strive to better themselves and discard anyone in the way. That is the way they are. I know because I was a small part in their puzzle doing their deeds.

Most wars are not for the good of the American people; they are for themselves and money but most of all power. I never understood why our young men had to die over countries that have been at war for thousands of years. Can't we just keep our nose out of it? The answer is simple: no! I truly believe this is why government agencies are formed and why they develop monsters like me. I didn't care for their cause or question why; I just did what I was told. This kid has to die and that is that, I thought. I don't care; what is one kid compared to the whole? Nothing.

Time was still counting down, and I was sitting there trying not to listen to his jabber. I just wanted this over. Yes, I am very impatient and just wanted to move on to the next task. I just wanted to go and break his damn neck to shut him up. But no, I had to keep waiting for the time. It had now been twenty-three minutes. Please hurry up, I thought. I am tired of hearing the begging and hearing about his family crap. Just let me kill him and get it over with.

I finally acknowledged him and said, "Kid, I don't know what you did to be here, but you are going to die when that clock runs out. If you have anything to say, go ahead and spill it out."

Again, he kept telling me he had no idea why he was here and why they wanted him to die. I told him, "Maybe because you should have kept your mouth shut and chosen another career instead of politics and evil government empire. Maybe you were just in the wrong place at the wrong time. I don't know, but they asked me to kill you, and that is what I intend to do."

Again, he begged me for his life. I'd seen movies where hitmen had similar experiences with people begging for their lives, and they always ended up dead. I guess it was because they put themselves in that position of life to end up there. If they'd never done anything wrong, they wouldn't have been there with a gun to their head. I figured the same with this kid. He did something, and it was time for him to die and suffer knowing that his demise was counting down on some red clock on the wall. That was all the time you had left of your life.

If you had one hour to think about the end of your life, what would you say? Knowing that begging did not help. Would you regret things? Would you tell the truth finally or take whatever it is to the grave? Just on the mere chance that you were let go, would you change your life?

I finally asked the kid, "What did you do? You don't have much time left; if you have something to say, then get it out. You are going to die. But at least go out with dignity and say what you need." I told him, "I would. What do you have to lose?"

To my surprise, he insisted on his innocence and kept trying to convince me that he was a good boy just trying to make it in life. It really did sound sincere. But again, I really didn't care all that much. I hate to say this, but I was getting excited to just snap his damn neck. I wanted to get on with the next test or whatever was coming.

Forty-one minutes had passed, and he was still at it, proclaiming his innocence and how much he loved his family and girlfriend. Telling me how he loved her and wished he would have asked her to marry him. I just told him, "Well, it's a little late now for that."

What came next kinda surprised me: he pissed his pants. I could see the yellow urine running on the floor. I guess he was truly scared. That was a good move on his part, I have to say. It added validity to his story of innocence. But again it did not change anything in my way of thinking. In fact, all I could think of was I hope I get a steak or lobster for doing this afterward. I was hoping for some type of reward. I know it's sick, but that is how I coped with things.

By this time I no longer saw him as a person, just a task at hand and what I needed to accomplish. Second by second, I sat there waiting for the time to run out so I could be out of that damn room and move on to something else or go back to my life for a while. Whatever, I was ready, and he was in my way to a steak dinner. Coldhearted? Yeah, I suppose, but what the hell did I care? My whole life was a mess, and nothing ever went my way. Life sucks.

Finally, ten minutes left, and we could end this jabbering crap and get on with it. Still, he kept claiming he was innocent, which by this time I didn't even care about. I just wanted out of the room, and in ten minutes I would be. I knew they wouldn't kill me because I was doing what they wanted, and for some strange reason they had put in here with him for a very long time. Maybe they were wanting him to confess or something. No idea, but my time in this shithole was about up. His time was definitely up.

Five minutes to that steak I was hoping for. I told the kid, "Confess and get it over with before you meet God, my friend." Again, he just sobbed and then started calling me names. Cussing me out for being a coward and shooting him tied up and so on. In one ear and out the other. I didn't care at this point.

I finally told him he had less than a minute of life left. At this time, he started telling his mom, dad, sisters, girlfriend that he loved them very much and would see them again. Blah blah blah.

"*Time is up!*" I said.

I stood up. I had no intention of shooting him. I wanted to make it more personal, and I was going to break his fucking neck for making me sit there so long listening to his crap. I'd started walking over to him when I heard the man on the speaker and another one who came into the room yelling at me. "Follow the orders and shoot him! That is what you were told to do!" Shit, they seemed pissed off at me for trying to go the extra mile.

"OK," I said.

I sat back down in the chair and grabbed the gun and put one in his chest. What the hell? I thought. It was a damn blank. I raised up to shoot again when the man in the room said, "That is enough. Put the gun down!"

"OK," I said, not understanding any of this.

At this time he went over and uncuffed the boy, and he stood up and said good job. What was this? He left the room, and the man told me to get up and follow him. Of course I did what was asked and just walked, wondering what the hell had just happened.

I was escorted again down the long corridor, and we walked in silence. I did ask the man (different than before), "What is going on?" Again no words came out of his mouth, and he just kept walking. I was so confused about this whole test. I just didn't get anything.

I was placed in a room with two chairs again and a table. I was praying I would not have to go through this again. My head was going crazy. Maybe that was the test, I thought, and now it's time for the real thing. Fuck, I just wanted to get the hell out of there. I hated not being talked to or knowing anything.

Of course, I could see cameras on the ceiling as they watched me, so I kept still and just sat there. It seemed like hours but more likely was just one hour. I sat and sat waiting for someone to come, and finally a well-dressed man came in with a notepad, and sat on the other side. Finally, some damn answers.

He sat for a few minutes just observing me before he ever spoke up. He didn't call me by my name ever! He told me that this was a test and I passed and that so many had failed before me. He asked me if I had any questions. I had thousands of them, I told him. "Like I don't understand any of this," I said.

He began telling me that in the life I was choosing, there would be times when these circumstances come into play when you have to take a life and they will always beg you and try to influence you as to why they don't

MONSTER

need to die. "They will lie, and they will try anything to get to you," the man said.

"We put you in there with one of our associates to make you feel uncomfortable and to play on your emotions to make you question that you shouldn't do this task," he continued. "We gave you no idea that he works with us, and the test was to see if you would follow through without question." He looked at me a moment. "It did surprise us when you decided on your own to break his neck. A little surprising…no one has ever done that before. But the task was to shoot him, not break his neck. From this point on, when you are given an order, follow the order."

Then he went on to ask me question about how I felt and if he had touched me in any way that made me question anything. I explained that getting to know the boy in the beginning really made it quite hard to kill him. "That was very difficult," I said. "Then when you tied him up and told me to shoot an unarmed boy for no reason, it really played hell with my emotions."

"That was all part of the plan," the man told me, "because there will be times you might be asked to kill one of your own. Maybe even someone you know. You cannot let emotions or feelings stand in your way. There is a reason for everything, and you must follow your orders whether you agree with them or not. We have our reasons."

He then asked why I chose to go through with it. I told him that I just wanted out of the room, I was sick of hearing about family, and I just wanted to leave and this was the way out. He said, "Good answer. But to kill a kid?"

I told him, "That is what you wanted me to do. I had no idea why, but you people wanted it done, and he must have done something to deserve it, so he had to go. I really just wanted to end it. I did not want to keep rethinking whether or not to do it. I just wanted to do it and forget about it."

The man just nodded his head in agreement. He then asked, "Why break his neck instead of shooting him?"

"I wanted to be an overachiever, I guess," I said. "Plus, I was just sick of hearing him and wanted to shut him up. I just wanted you people to understand that I didn't need a gun to kill someone—I could do it with my hands and make it more personal and finish the mission. I wanted to make sure you all knew that I was your guy without question."

He then asked me what they could have done differently to make me not want to finish it. I had to think about this for a while. I guessed they wanted to keep upgrading the test to make it harder and harder to make people second-guess themselves.

I told him the boy's innocence really got me. The pissing of the pants really got me. The family got me. All of that was really good and did make me question a lot of things. I guessed the only thing that would have maybe made me really question it was if he would have been a young marine. That would have been against all my morals and pride. "I don't know if I could have done that one," I said. "Marines are a brotherhood, and seeing a young marine losing his life to me…not sure if I could have done that."

He just sat back and looked at me. "Never heard that answer before," he stated. "Very good one, in fact. I do know that you all share a bond, a bond tighter than the rest of the military. As you stated, a brotherhood. Not sure we ever looked at a scenario that holds something ingrained in the DNA of military people. Hmm," he said looking at me.

Then of course I could see the next question coming. "So maybe your next test will be with a young marine from your home state that just got out of boot camp, and then we will see if you can finish that mission."

I looked down in sadness and said, "Please don't ask that of me. I promise to do whatever you ask, but please don't do that to me. That is something I might never be able to forgive myself for. I really hope you people are not that cruel."

He sat back and looked at me again in silence. I was really dreading bringing that up. Please, God, don't make me do something like that, I thought. I just can't do it, nor do I want part of an organization that would make a person do that.

We sat across the table and just looked at each other.

He then piped up, saying "Don't worry; we are not here to kill the innocents. We are here to protect our way of life. However, there may be times when you are asked to kill those military people that are rogue and working with our enemies. Would that be OK with you?"

I stated, "Yes, I understand that completely." I finally relaxed.

He then asked me, "Are you able to turn off your feelings and emotions and go back to work as though nothing has happened—after a mission, of course?

"Of course," I said, "because in my mind I am helping out Americans and doing what is asked of me."

He nodded in agreement. He asked again, "What if you are wounded or die?"

I stated, "I have already died in my mind, so I don't care. At least I would die for my country and hopefully saving the innocents."

I told him that I was bored in my life and that I should have died in the Gulf War with my friends. I told him I was ready for anything and death was not something I wasn't afraid of anymore. "I know I have my children," I said, "but they are with their mother and will be better off without me anyway. I'm just a blank person with no life and nothing to really live for anyway. I could never find happiness in this life, and I never knew kindness of any kind. People are horrible: they cheat, they lie, they are no good. I do not like people much; I think people's honor is dead. There are no good people in this life, only misery."

His next question caught me off guard. He asked, "Do you believe in God?"

Wow. I told him I thought I'd found him at one point in my life. However, this life is so cruel that surely if he was a benevolent God, then wouldn't there be some good people in this life? "Why is there only misery, and war?" I asked. "It seems from the beginning of time there has been war. There is no love for thy other man. Only what can I get from him and give nothing back. People use people all the time, and never once do they actually want to repay a good deed that was done to them. People are horrible, and really if you look hard at people, there is no good. Maybe just a small part, the rest is evil, and what they can do to hurt you or use you. Even the holiest of people like priests' rape kids. These are people that are there to teach us of God and his kindness but yet in the dark hurt our children. What kind of life is this? I will be honored to kill anyone, because they all deserve to die. Including myself. I am no better than they are."

I think that really grabbed him. Not sure if he liked my answer or not, but that is how I truly feel. A Chinese man once told me that a friend is like an enemy in disguise. Translated, that means that if someone out there hates you and doesn't really know you, you don't really care. However, when a family or friend betrays you, it kills you inside and rips your heart out. That is because you are emotionally tied to that person and they know your deepest secrets, and when you are betrayed, it kills you. Trust is a hard thing to find, but if you ever find someone you can, embrace them. They are truly a rare breed and not many of them out there. Most just want to gossip and hurt you indirectly. I am tired of these people. "I am ready for whatever is next, if you so choose," I told him.

I looked over at him and just gave a mean and hateful look. He looked at me and said, "You have a very ugly outlook on life."

I asked him if he thought different, and if he did, could he explain it to me so I could understand. He sat in silence for a minute, I guess to think about my question to him.

"What happens if there are good people out there?" he finally asked. "Honest, loving, hardworking, God-fearing people out there?" Apparently, he actually thought there are.

I said,

He again said, "What happens if there are? Would you be the sheepdog and protect them? Would you give a child a chance to try and be that person? Would you want to give him the best chance in life to prove you wrong? Would you?"

I sat in deep silence and almost wept. I really did want to believe in humanity; I really did. I just had such a shitty life that I could not see past it. I nodded in agreement and said, "Yes, I would protect them with my life. I would want to protect the innocent and give them a chance to do better than I. I want to believe that I am wrong. I want more than anything to find out that my life is not the normal."

He said, "There are people out there like this, and you can make a difference. You can be that one guy that makes a difference."

Again, I felt like crying. Big tough marine wanted to cry at that particular moment. Very sad for me. Keep on task on what you are doing and one day *you* will make the difference. However, you must trust us in what we say and do as you are asked to a T. No diversion. You will make a difference, although you may never know what difference you make, but you will have made a difference in your life. Yes, God will know what you have done for humanity, and you will be praised in the hereafter for your work.

I nodded my head and realized this was my time to do as I was told and become the monster they wanted me to become. I needed to save people even if they didn't know I existed. I am no one but an apparition in their peripheral vision, I thought. But I am there, and I will destroy all those with great vengeance to hopefully help that one person that can make a difference in their lives.

By then the conversation was about over. He told me to eat my crappy dinner and soon I would be going back to work. He said, "You've done well; your answers are great, and you will make a difference in this life. Not only will God be proud of you, but so will America."

Little did I know that they are so damn smart they understood how to brainwash me and get me to go all in 100 percent. These people truly are the masters of grooming you to go in and kill or be killed and love every minute of it. They knew what to touch and how to influence me. I am still to this day brainwashed, thinking what I did was for the good. But in my heart, I know what I have done was not for the good but for greed.

After I ate, they brought in a gurney and told me to lie down; it was time to go to sleep, and when I woke up, it would be time to go home and wait till the next time they came. I did what they asked, they stuck a needle in me, and off to sleep I went.

Chapter 3

TEST TWO: SKILL TEST

Time went on like it always does. I was not sure what was coming next, if anything, although I felt like I had done what they asked and felt like they would challenge me again. At least I was hoping.

It had been about a month, and I was doing my job on the rig, working and learning to be more proficient. I kinda just sat looking at everything, thinking about what had happened and wondered endlessly when the next test would arrive. I knew in a few days that I would be flying home and was hoping to see my boys and spend some time with them.

Time finally arrived, and I was on the plane flying back home. I didn't know whether or not I would be drugged out and tested or just allowed to have some time off. Not really sure but was hoping in my heart to go through another test. After the plane landed, I went to the baggage area to get my bags. I paused to look around, waiting for them to come and get me. Nothing!

This really played with my head; I'd thought for sure I was their guy, but maybe not. I went home and drove over to see my boys and just relax, I guess. I spent about two weeks with them and then drove back home to spend the rest of the time hanging out and resting up waiting to go back to Africa.

After about three days at home, I received a phone call and was told to dress in regular attire and go to the airport, and there would be a ticket for me. The man on the phone also said no need for any extra clothes or anything; everything would be provided. Just put my truck in a long-term parking lot and get on the plane, and they would pick me up in Houston.

I have to admit I was really excited that I would be tested again and maybe one day make the team. So I got in my truck with nothing extra, just some cash, and went to the airport. I remembered them pounding into my head, "Do what you are told only." So I did nothing extra—no extra clothes, no toothbrush, no nothing—just drove, got on the plane, and went to Houston. I was so excited to say the least.

After arriving in the airport, I was not sure what to do then or where to go. I didn't have any further details. So I just got off the plane and looked around and headed for the luggage, even though I didn't have any. I figured they could find me if they wanted to. I was right; they were there in regular clothing and looked very normal. They came up to me and told me to follow them, and so I did. We went into the parking lot and got into a car and drove off. I sat in the back while the two up front didn't say a word to me or to each other. How awkward. I figured they wouldn't talk to me but to each other. But no, they didn't even look at each other or bother to look back at me. I felt like this is horseshit. But yet this has been their demeanor the whole time with me. They never say shit and barely look at me and nothing else. Maybe a single word is all I might get. These guys really know how to make a person feel uncomfortable.

We finally arrived in a parking lot with a blacked-out SUV; one of the guys opened the door for me. I got out and the door to the SUV opened, and so I proceeded to walk over and get in. Now the weird part again.

One driver, one passenger, and one guy in the back. He opened his bag of goodies and took out a needle and grabbed my arm. Oh shit, here we go again. Now what? I thought. Yes, out I go.

I had no idea where I was when I woke up. I saw a couple of bags on the floor, a dirty-ass window and room, and it was hot and muggy. I saw an old dirty shower with a dirty-ass towel hanging there and some bags of food of some kind with two bottles of water.

I made it over to the window with my new headache, not having any idea of how long I had been out or how long it had been. I looked out and saw that I was in some kind of city or town, I guess. Looked like I was in the middle of some Mexican or Hispanic village; I was not sure where I was at all. I didn't even look in the bags yet, just went to the shitty-ass food and water and ate and drank it all. I must have been out for a while. I had no idea how long it had been or anything. Like I said, I had no damn clue where I was. I did know somewhere in South America.

It was time to look into the bags of crap and see what they had for me and what I was supposed to do. I put everything on the bed and spread everything out. The list of items follows:

1. Pistol with silencer and four mags
2. Single-action rifle with fifteen rounds
3. Big knife
4. Map with compass
5. GPS with coordinates in there
6. Clothes: socks, shoes, belt underwear, pants, shirt, long thin coat (waterproof and camo), a poncho (camo)
7. Letter
8. Money
9. Ticket and return
10. Lighter
11. Camelback
12. Paracord

I opened the letter, and this is all I got from it. Take a shower, put your new clothes on. Leave your old clothes in the room—do not take anything you came; with leave all behind. Put your gear in the bag and leave for the train station and take the ticket to your destination. Once you get to your new area, use the GPS and follow the map to your destination. You will be out in the jungle; it will take you approximately two to three days depending on what you encounter before you reach your target. Approximately fifteen to twenty-five personnel will be there. You will destroy all life and return back to motel. Note anything you encounter that you deem a threat; eliminate at your discretion. You will also need to bring all your gear back, place in bag at hotel, and wait for further instruction. After you read this, leave the letter and move out.

I guess it was time to move. I filled up the camelback with water, and to my surprise, there were protein bars in there. That was a surprise. These guys are not thoughtful at all; they are just horrible people, so to speak.

I got down on the street and saw a vender selling bottles of water. I thought to myself, I better change out the water so I don't get the shits. The last thing I wanted was this and not being able to finish the mission. I also grabbed some candies so I could get some sugar in me and help with the headaches. I asked one of the guys where the choo-choo train was. He just laughed, thinking I was some dumbass tourist.

I made my way to the train depot and gave my ticket; he showed me a sign that said it would be there in a few hours. This really sucked. I sat down and fired up the GPS to see how far I was away from the spot; it showed that I had about 143 miles to go. It looked from the GPS that I had about 122 miles on the train and 21 miles through the jungle. I thought to myself, This isn't going to take me two to three days. Hell, I could make that in fifteen hours at best—so I thought.

MONSTER

In the military, I'd done lots of jungle training, and this was surely not going to be that difficult, but who cares? If they gave me that much time, I would just take my time and get it done.

After sitting there for a while, I started thinking about what they'd asked me to do. Was I really supposed to kill all these people, or was this another trick? Not really sure what it was, but for some reason they wanted me to do this, and I was going to fulfill it. I knew that I only had so many rounds to accomplish the task, so I had to be careful not to use them up and make sure every round counted. If someone was left alive, then I should use the knife, not a round. I also started thinking of using the knife as much as I could to conserve the rounds till I had no choice. That would be the better option. Better yet, use their weapons and save mine for an emergency.

I couldn't open the map because there were too many around, and I didn't want to be seen. I just wanted to fit in like a tourist, and that was it—even though I had a bag full of weapons. I just wanted to make it there and come back.

I wasn't sure if I was overthinking this or what, but I realized that I would be out in the jungle for days, so I thought I better buy as much water as I can carry. I can find water in most places in the jungle, but why not help out the situation if I can? I am sure they have plenty of water at my destination, and food. LOL.

As I sat there waiting on the train, I remember a man from this part of the country sitting next to me. He started talking to me in English asking, me where I was going and where I was from. I didn't dare ask him what country I was in; that would have made him question me, letting on that I didn't even know where I was. I just made small talk like a dumb tourist and said "USA" and "just traveling to see the country." I was hoping he would just shut up and leave me alone. But again, I didn't want to be rude and needed to fit in and not look out of place.

Again he started telling me he always wanted to go to the USA and see Las Vegas. I just nodded. He asked me if I'd ever been there. I told him yes, once, and just leaned back like I was tired, hoping he would get the hint and leave me alone. Then he started in again, saying I should go see this and that. I had no idea what the hell he was talking about. I just said, "Wherever the train takes me is where I will see." He looked at me like I was some kind of weirdo. But I didn't really care. He asked if I had anything from America that he could buy from me as a souvenir.

I just told him no. He asked, "What about in the bag? Can I buy one of your old shirts or something?"

I said, "No, I need my clothes." I especially didn't want to open my bag for him since it was full of weapons. I was really getting annoyed with this guy.

Of course, he followed up with another question. If I wanted a girlfriend, he knew some ladies in the next town he could help me out with.

Fuck! Leave me alone. I told him not interested.

He then said, "All you Americans like girls from here. Come on—hang out with me for a day or two. You will have a good time."

I said again, "No, not interested." I then told him, "If you don't mind, I need to rest. I am very tired and want to just sit here. However, I really enjoyed our conversation."

I had my foot through the loop of the bag just in case someone tried to snatch and grab. But all was good. I sat there for another hour or so, and the train showed up. I picked up the bag, nodded to the guy, and went in and sat down. Now this was no treasure chest of any kind. It was dirty and stinky, and I wanted to puke.

After an eternity of sitting there with people trying to talk to me and me being nice, this was my reward? *Yuck*. I just wanted to check my GPS and see how far I had come and how far I had to go. I finally got a good signal and saw that I had about ten miles to go before I turned off into the jungle. However, I wasn't sure when the next stop would be, and I wasn't about to jump off this train.

I would have to stay on until it slowed down or stopped. Now I thought I understood why it was going to take me a few days. They were right, and I was stupid. I'd never really figured that into the equation, but so be it.

After the ten miles came and went, I was like, fuck me when is the next stop? About thirteen miles past the area, the train came to a small village, and that is where I got off. Now I understood completely. Didn't have twenty-one miles; I had thirty-four miles to walk. Shit, this sucks ass. I got off at the town and looked like a dumbass in the middle of bum fuck Egypt. I took out some money and bought a little food and grabbed some more water.

I went to the edge of the town, turned on my GPS in a nice and secluded place, and looked at my destination. I thought about walking down the tracks or going straight from my location. I looked at the map and saw my heading from where I was at. Just in case my batteries ran out, I had a compass, which I am very proficient at using.

The map had contours on it, so I could see that this was really not the way I wanted to go. So I looked on the map and followed the train track to see if I could bypass the rivers and maybe get around some of the mountains. It all looked like crap. No matter which way I went, I would have lots of obstacles in the way. So I figured by looking at the map that my best chance was walking down the tracks for about six miles and then cutting into the jungle. The route didn't look that much better, but at least there weren't so many obstacles in my way.

This led to another thought: Who in the hell would be out in this crap so far away from town? In the middle of the jungle really. This can't be. I opened up the GPS and zoomed out and saw a road that was maybe one mile from the destination. Now that made more sense. However, I knew better than to take a road to somewhere like a drug or gun ring. I thought really hard about this. Maybe if I walked at night, I could be undetected. Stupid idea. They would surely have the road watched if they were drug or gun people, wouldn't they? Better idea is go into the jungle and make my way to them. This is the safer bet and really the only one. Unless I stole a car and drove it there and parked past the place…

Stupid. I was just being lazy and not wanting to go through the jungle.

I always believe it's best to go with your gut, so with that said, off to the tracks I went and started my ass walking.

I walked and walked in this humid shithole of a country, still wondering why these people were to die. What did they do to have our government want them dead? I had many thoughts about this, and the only conclusions I could come up with were drugs or guns. Only things that I could think of.

I finally came to my point of interest where I would cut into the jungle and head for that long-ass walk. I was not really looking forward to jungle walking, but this was the job and I did have plenty of experience in this type of terrain. So I ventured in and got myself a hundred yards in or so with 22.5 miles to walk. Time for camouflage and concealment. Now this I know very well; I know how to blend in quite well.

I put down my bag of weapons and dug out my paracord and took about three or four feet of it. If you cut the end, there are tiny strands that are very strong in there, and you can use them more efficiently than just the big strand. So I cut them up and started cutting off leaves with branches. Nothing big but I had to break up my outline as best as I could. See, a person's outline is very easy to distinguish anywhere, but if you add things to the body, it becomes much more difficult to make you out. The only downside is that it can get snagged or make additional noise. But avoiding that comes with experience and being able to move as one with extensions.

After about an hour or so, I was ready to start. I turned on the GPS, got my direction, and from here on out planned to use the compass as much as possible to conserve the batteries in the GPS. I needed that to pinpoint the target. Off I went.

Before I started, it was important to know what to expect in a jungle. Very hot, humid, lots of pooling water, waterfalls, lots of food varieties, and you are always wet. Now the animals can be dangerous too. Lots of snakes, poisonous ants, and poisonous plants, so one must know the terrain and move slowly and cautiously.

The first little while, the walk was very relaxing. The sounds in the jungle can be both scary and yet very soothing. I was enjoying moving through the jungle and trying to keep a heading. It really is impossible to move in a straight line, but if you have a good heading, you can move through obstacles and get back on course rather easily. Of course it depends on the size of the obstacles.

I was about two hours into the jungle and figured I had moved about one and half miles in, which wasn't that bad, considering it was the jungle. But at this pace it was going to take me a while. Again I had a few days to do it. The main problem was moving at night with no vision. It becomes increasingly difficult to see at night, especially because of the overcast of trees. I still had some good light, so I was trying to move as fast and smoothly as I could.

A few miles in, I came upon a path. Now, go figure—this must be a path for the locals to come in from town or wherever and gather items or hunt, I guessed.

MONSTER

Even though the path was not well used, it was a path that most people would follow. Not I, for sure. I knew most paths can be booby-trapped or watched, and I had no intention of following it. So I just took my own path and kept trucking along.

I came across the most wonderful scenery, almost breathtaking. Whether it was the constant waterfalls or the rock terrain or the animals, it was just gorgeous and beautiful. A person could spend his or her whole life in the jungle and never get bored. I saw monkeys of all different kinds; I even saw a sloth. I stayed there and just looked at him. I believe it was the first one I'd ever seen. I was thinking of Ice Age sloths. I wanted to laugh, but I knew I couldn't. What a beautiful jungle I was in, so peaceful and euphoric. The only animal I wasn't sure about was the jaguar. Not something I wanted to run into, but I did have a few weapons on me.

By now I was probably four or five miles in and moving quite nicely. Nighttime was on its way, and my eyes were adjusting but not quite enough. I also knew that nighttime is really the best time to move as long as you don't get hurt. At night you can hear everything and see anyone with a fire (camp). I did have a feeling that I would run into locals and wasn't sure what to do if I did. But again, I would cross that path when it came up.

Nighttime was here, and I was slowing down and moving very slow. I wasn't all that tired, so I wanted to make as much progress as I could. I was very anxious to see what my prospects looked like and how many were in there. I prayed there were no kids. Women? Oh well, wrong place and wrong time, I guess.

It was time to turn on the GPS and see how far I was off. I was moving faster than I'd thought; I was sixteen miles from target. Tomorrow I would surely be close enough to smell them or hear them. But again, I was not tired and I had veered off a bit, so I took another reading and got back on track.

Wasn't more than a mile farther when I heard something in the distance that sounded like people. I couldn't even believe my ears—like what the hell were they doing out here? I kept a slower pace to try and get a visual on them. I saw a nice cliff breaking through the trees, so that was where I headed to see if I could see something. Believe me, it took some time to scale that thing without breaking my neck. But I finally made it. To my surprise there were a few small huts in the distance. I could see a couple of fires and people. I guessed it was another small village off some road that was not on my map. I sunk down in some bushes and took another GPS reading to find out where they were so I could mark it on the map for the travel home.

I wish I could have seen it in daylight; I imagine it was a beautiful place to camp. However, I needed to get away from this so I was not seen. It would not be good to be seen in the jungle after a massacre.

The night grew long, and I grew tired. I traveled maybe another mile or so trying to get away from the village. I found a really beautiful spot where I could try and catch a few hours of sleep. It was in a group of trees with a gorgeous opening in the middle. I could see the sky and stars on this night. Very peaceful and very quiet. I cleared out some of the underbrush and made a nice little spot for a sleep. I put my backpack down and used it as a pillow, then grabbed some water and a bite to snack on. Soon I was fast asleep.

I woke up throughout the night, probably because the jungle was full of noise and because of the event I was going to. I often wonder if they told the people I was coming just to see if I was good enough to kill them hunting me. I honestly didn't know what to expect, especially from the government after the last test. Was I really supposed to kill these people, or was there some other test I didn't know about? Anyway, I had my orders, and off I went.

I walked for several hours and didn't run into anyone or even hear anyone. I was relieved. I really didn't want to be compromised and have to kill someone because they saw me. Plus, I still wasn't sure if the bullets were blanks or real. This did really bother me. I was lost in thoughts.

I sat down and took a drink and ate a bar and turned on the GPS to gain another heading. To my surprise, I was within a few miles of the objective. I knew it was time to be quiet now. I had 2.2 miles to go, so I was getting really close. Now came the question do I attack at night or wait till the morning? That answer was clear. I was going to wait till about 2:00 a.m. and go in. The only way I could take down that many people was at night and quietly.

I slowly walked to my objective. I had to see what I was dealing with and how many I was looking at. After a time, I was finally within a few hundred yards of them, and I could hear them yelling and laughing and women in the background. I was not happy with this; I'd never really killed a woman before and prayed there were no kids. I just couldn't do that, not even for them. I think they know that about me, I thought, but we will see.

As I advanced up, I found a nice tree to hide behind where I could see the village. It was in plain sight. I sat for a while and just counted. I figured about nine males and three or four women and no kids. The good thing was they were all drinking and having a great time. This meant they would pass out and I could make my way in and just use a knife and be more undetected. As I sat there, I could feel the rush coming into my body; the adrenaline was flowing fast and furious. I honestly couldn't wait to do this and start my journey back home.

It was about midnight when they finally were heading to bed. I still waited for another hour until I didn't see any movement. It was time to go in and make my kills and show this government my skill set.

I took off most of my cover so I could move in without obstruction and be quick and precise. I made it to the first cabin. Looking in, I saw four men lying in the beds. I backed off of this one because I needed a smaller kill first. I thought I would save these men for last because if they woke up, I would have to use one of the guns. There was four of them, I was not sure I could kill them all with a knife without waking others up. So I moved on.

The next hut I came to was just right. Only a man and a woman in there. Both sleeping nicely. I moved into the hut using the wall as my cover so I wouldn't move into the open floor and break up my outline. When I was over top of them, I slit the man's neck just right to bleed him out. Of course he woke up with my hand over his mouth. His eyes were big like he just saw a ghost. He started kicking a little, and the woman just moved over, never waking up. This was great. Once he bled out, I just did the same thing to her. I went to her side and stuck her right in the artery. I put my hand over her mouth and just shushed her. I watched as her eyes screamed in terror. This was a little different. I could feel her blood spurting on my hand and arm. How warm it was, like no other feeling, really. I was truly enjoying this.

Both of them were dead as hell. It was time to see what was next. This was very quiet and smooth. I made my way over to another hut. This guy must have been the boss. He was in bed with two women. Lucky bastard. Well, not tonight. He had to go first, of course, then both of the women. I made my way over to them, and all were sound asleep. I reached over one of the women because his fat ass was in the middle of them. I stabbed him in the neck and put my hand over his mouth. He started kicking and screaming in my hand. The woman closest to me woke up, to my surprise. The other did not. I immediately took my knife and slit her throat from one end to the other. This would certainly stop her from screaming. Just a nice slow gurgling sound, and that was it. The man was soon falling asleep with the blood leaving his body fast. Well, two down and one more to go. I just walked over to the other woman and stuck my knife right through her chest. I really don't know why I did this and not the neck. I knew I hit the heart because it wasn't long before she was dead. I stood back and looked at them for a while; I guess I was just proud of myself for a job so far well done.

I found another guy sleeping out by the fire. All alone, oh goodie. This was easy. I simply walked up behind him and slit his throat from end to end. Easy peasy. I could hear the gurgling sound, so I tilted his head down over his chest to hide the noise. Worked perfectly. He was dead now. Three women and three men gone. That was six total. I had at least one more woman and seven or eight men.

I found my way to another hut. This time there were three men sleeping in there. I decided to pass on this and see what was in the last hut. I moved in, and to my surprise there were only two men and no women. Huh, I thought maybe there was another woman, but I guess not.

I simply walked over to one sleeping on his back and slit his throat and held him with my hands over his mouth very tightly. Not much sound, but this pig took a while to bleed out. Not happy with this. I kept waiting for the other man to wake up. I really didn't want to use my weapon. I did not want a gunfight if I could avoid it. The first man finally died out.

Now it was time to try something new. I had three or four guys in each of the next two huts and wasn't sure how I was going to kill them without waking up the others. So while I was out in the woods, I took some of the paracord and tied on two sticks. This was a method the Vietnam vets used that I had never tried. So the second man in the hut was the guinea pig. He was on his side, which actually made it easier. I slowly put the cord around his neck and tightened it. To my surprise, it was not a good and quiet tactic at all. He flayed around and kicked. Although he did not make a whole lot of sound, still he was not happy. I kept it on him for a while until it was over with. I thought to myself, Not using this thing again. It just gave him too much time to kick and knock shit over. This is not the right atmosphere for this type of killing technique.

Now it was time for the remaining seven men. I was not sure how to do this without using a weapon. For some reason I wanted to go back with all the ammo like it was nothing. I could use the pistol in just a second, and it would be done. But that seemed too easy. So I decided I would just stick the men with the knife and try and do it the old-fashioned way for now. If I needed the weapon, I surely had it to use.

As I made my way back to the three-person tent, I got lucky again. One of the men was taking a piss. This was a great opportunity to make his life a little more exciting. I made my way to him using an old military trick. I would not look at his head because he would have the feeling of being watched and look back. So I stared at his waist so that he wouldn't have the feeling yet I could see his body if he did try and turn around. It worked beautifully. He never had any idea I was behind him. I reached up and slit his throat and bent his head down over his chest and listened to the quiet gurgling sound. Almost like a waterfall in the jungle. How pleasant it was. I could also feel the blood oozing from his neck onto my arm. How nice and warm it was. It wasn't long and he was out.

Now I just had two to deal with in the hut. As I came in, to my surprise one of the men was getting up to piss, I assume, and was coming straight at me. I was standing next to the wall when I thrust forward and stuck him in the solar plexus up to his heart. It was over in a matter of seconds. I laid him down softly and made my way over to the sleeping guy. I just casually walked over and stuck him right in the artery and watched his eyes stare at me with a scared and begging look. Oh well, no mercy here, I thought. Just hurry up and die, will you.

Now I had to do the big task: four men in close order combat. I now knew how I had to do this. They were all in one room, so it had to be quick, and I didn't care if they made noise since there was no one left. I crept over to the first guy and slit his throat fast, cutting his head almost completely off with one quick swipe. I jumped to the other bed and did the same. By this time the other two were waking up, wondering what was happening. The third guy sat up and was looking at me when I cut his throat down to the neck bone. By this time the other guy had jumped up and So, was running toward me. This was easy. I stuck him so hard in the abdomen and sliced him down to his groin. He let out a yell, and I pulled out the knife and sliced his throat like warm butter. I stepped back and was so proud of myself. No bullets and all were dead.

Well, so I thought. When I came out of the hut, the fourth woman, whom I'd thought wasn't there, was standing in front of me with her hands over her mouth, crying. She got on her knees and started in with the tears, begging for her life. Well, in Spanish. I assume that was what she was doing. I walked over to her and grabbed her hair and snapped her neck with ease. I had a mission and I really didn't care. For some reason they'd wanted them all dead, and they were all dead now.

I decided to make one more pass to make sure it was all secure. It was; no one was left alive. Now I needed to decide how to get back: Do I take a vehicle or motorcycle or walk back through the jungle? It was my decision. However, I was covered in blood—not a good way to go back to the train station. I hadn't really considered this. But I was now.

I needed new clothes, and I needed to wash all this blood off me. I knew I could find some because some of the men were really fat and I could fit nicely in their clothes. So I went around and gathered some stuff up and went over to their well water. It was a five-hundred-gallon black tank on a trailer full of water. I stripped down and started to wash. I was so glad they had soap waiting there for me. How nice of them, I thought.

I finally got cleaned up and put on their clothes. It was nice to feel clean again and have some new attire. It was about 4:00 a.m. at this time. And I decided to take a motorcycle to the train and follow the road. I was hoping there were no roadblocks in the road, but my gut was telling me there weren't. I have always been a firm believer that you should follow your gut. I know, I know—I should have made my way through the jungle. But if someone found them, they would be looking for me. So I needed to get back to the motel as quickly as possible.

I grabbed a motorcycle and put my backpack on and kept my sidearm in my belt on my stomach under a fat man's clothes. Off I went down the road to the village. After only a little time, I found myself outside the village where the train station was. I saw people moving around, and I parked the bike and decided to walk in just like some damn stupid tourist. I made my way over to the station having no idea when the train was coming or when they would open. I was hoping soon, though. I was ready to get back with a big shit-eating grin on my face like "Yeah, that was easy; what is next?" Ha-ha.

It was now completely morning, and I was just sitting there eating a protein bar and drinking some water like nothing had happened. Very proud of myself. It was about 8:00 a.m. when I saw some other people coming to the train station. I thought this was a good sign. Wasn't long after that I saw the window open, and I walked up to give him my ticket. He told me to wait and the train would be there around nine or so. So I went back and sat down. The next hour was really the hardest for me. I kept waiting for someone to start screaming that the people were dead and for people to start looking for me. Ticktock, ticktock. Damn train—wish it would get here! Not like I didn't stick out. Finally I could hear it coming; this was a big relief.

I made my way onto the train and sat quietly, waiting for it to start moving. This seemed to take forever, but in reality it was maybe twenty minutes. We were off, and

I knew just how many stops to get back to the hotel. I was so relieved that we were off and running back. The mission was about over, and I did not have a clue what to expect when I did make it back. I wondered if there would be a debriefing like after the other test or what they would say or do. I hoped I'd done it all correctly and that I was good.

I finally made it to my stop. Thank goodness. I made my way to the hotel and walked up to my room. To my surprise, it looked like no one had even been there. By this time I was really hungry, so I thought I would clean up and put my clothes back on and have a nice lunch. Of course, a nice crap and shower first. So I did just that. I went down in the court room and had a nice lunch and sat there. Then I decided to have a drink. One drink just to calm my excitement down a bit. But one turned into two, and two turned into three. I finally quit after feeling a little woozy. Thought it was time to go back to the hotel and get some well-deserved sleep.

I walked into the room, and of course someone was there. Shit, I wanted to sleep. He told me to leave everything and come with him. So I left all the gear except for the clothes I had on. We made our way down the stairs and into an old shitty car with a driver. Of course, no talking, just three of us driving somewhere.

We drove to an airport where a nice small jet was parked. I walked into the plane and sat down. Again, no one was even looking at me or talking to me. I didn't really like this silence crap, but I knew that was their way.

The man I came with opened his bag, and out came the needle. Fuck, here we go again," I thought But at least I would get some sleep. It wasn't long before I fell asleep again. This time when I woke up, I was in a hotel room in the States—or so I assumed because it was really nice with lots of food, and my clothes were all washed and ready for me to get dressed in. So I showered and put on my clothes and ate. After I was done eating, I turned on the TV because I was still not feeling all that well from the drugs. I fell back asleep, until I woke up to see a man—the same fucking man who interrogated me last time—was sitting there. I knew what this was about. He started in.

He asked me if I finished the mission? I told him yes; it was all done. He asked if anyone was left alive. I told him no, to the best of knowledge they were all dead. He then said, "You didn't use any bullets?" I told him no, I wanted to try and do it quietly for my escape. He said that was probably good thinking but was surprised that I could get away with using only a knife. He said that was a good tactic and very surprising I could accomplish this. I just told him the military taught me well. He nodded.

He then asked how I felt doing this. I lied a little and just told him that it was a mission, and I didn't pay it much mind. He stopped and looked into my eyes for a moment. He then said, "I don't think so. I think it either bothered you, or you're some kind of psycho."

I was caught, I thought. No lying to these people. So I told him the women did bother me, and I was very glad that no children were involved.

MONSTER

The man just sat there looking at me for some time. He then asked what would have happened if there were children involved? I told him frankly, "I am glad there weren't, and I do not know what I would have done. Children are innocent," I said, "and I hope never to be put in that situation. I am not a hungry psycho that would enjoy that.

He kept pressing me. "Well, what if there were; could you have killed them?"

I asked him politely, "Do I really have to answer that?"

He stated, Yes you do!"

"I guess I would have to see them as a threat of my life or my security," I said. "If they were, then yes, I would. If not, then I guess I couldn't. I would have to assess the situation at that time. Not sure what I would do."

He nodded at that answer. Then came the next question: "Is this the first woman you ever killed?" He knew that answer already.

"Yes," I answered.

Again with the question: "And how did that feel?"

"I saw them as a threat, and they had a choice to be there, so it was their choice to be there, and I took them out."

He then looked at me and said, "Were all of them a threat?"

I thought, Holy shit, do they know about the last one? I again reiterated they were all threats. "My life was more important than theirs," I said. "They must have done something wrong for you to send me in."

Again he sat back and looked deeply into me. He then told me that this was a test of my skills and to see if I could follow all the direction that was sent to me. They also had wanted to see how I went in and executed the mission and my way to get out. It was apparent that I did well and made good decisions.

I was a little relieved. I spoke up and asked him about the man at the train station. Was he in on this? He said, "Of course he was; he was there to make you nervous and see your reaction to his questions. Because this will always happen to you being a foreigner."

Then I proceeded to ask, "Why them?"

He told me first it was to score me on my skills. "Next, these particular people rob and take from other villages, and they just fit the criteria of what we needed to test you on. These people seem to cause violence to their neighbors and take what isn't theirs. They needed elimination, so to speak. Great task for you." He then asked, "How do you feel now?"

I just looked at him and said, "Relieved."

He asked, "What does that mean?"

"I am grateful to take out the trash," I told him. "They needed to die, and now I have the reason. I am glad for that."

Again, he sat back and looked at me. "Maybe you need a reason to kill someone?"

I told him, "It sure helps, but no, if you feel they need it, then I am just the pawn to do it. It's really not my place to question you people but just do my job and shut up. I really don't care as long as you all have your reasons."

MONSTER

He seemed pleased with my answers. He told me they would be in touch, and it was time to get back to work for a while. So he left with my ticket on the table and was gone.

Chapter 4

TEST 3A FINAL: NAVIGATIONS/ SURVIVAL (ISOLATION MOUNTAINS)

Well, life went on again. Once again, I was back working, and everything seemed to be normal. It had been about three months with time off and enjoying my boys and working. I now realize that they gave me time to recuperate and learn my so-called profession. Didn't realize that before, but of course they did.

It was time for me to fly back and see the boys and spend some time at home. Or so I thought. Once again, I flew into the airport and met up with the gentlemen. It was the same routine: I got in the car and the needle came out and off I went. I was really getting tired of all of this. Never knowing what I was doing, never really anyone to talk to except at the end. What now? I thought.

MONSTER

This was a totally different game or test. I woke up in the middle of the mountains in the cold. I was really freezing my ass off. Of course, there was a note, and here we go again. Of course I wondered, Where the hell am I and now what is expected of me?

The note went like this: This is a test of your land navigation skills and survival. You are given a map, a protractor, and a compass. You have very little food. You have a backpack with some items in there for survival. You need to find each point of interest, and in those points of interest you will receive the next assignment. This will be a long test and total isolation. There will be no contact with anyone, and you will have to finish the test to the best of your ability. If you fail to find any of the points, then I suggest you go back to the last point of interest and retrace your steps. You have no time limit to finish this course. Whether you finish or not is up to you. There will be a device if you quit; you are to push, and you will be brought out and fail, of course. Good luck with your journey.

OK, I thought. Navigation was easy for me. Well, I thought it was. I opened my bag of goodies, and this is the list of items:

1. Backpack with water full camelback
2. Big knife
3. One hundred feet of paracord
4. Poncho and liner
5. One box of matches
6. Magnifying glass (for starting fire, I presumed)

7. No change of clothes, just a nice heavy coat
8. Hat
9. Sunglasses
10. Gloves
11. Compass, protractor, and three different maps (the maps had a spot marked on them stating the first point)
12. Fifteen protein bars
13. One 45 caliber with three mags
14. One 308 rifle with ten rounds

Well, this shouldn't be too bad except for the cold, I thought. I looked at the first point that I needed to go to. It appeared to be about eleven miles away. I can do that, I thought. So, I packed up my stuff and wished I had a GPS, but that was OK. I could do it the old-fashioned way.

I looked around and saw huge mountains and realized that I had to cross one of them. That really sucked, especially if I was going to head in a straight line to find the point. I knew where my location was, so I could always shoot an intersection or resection to find out where I needed to go or where I was. This is how a resection is done: You take two known points and then use your compass and deflection and shoot azimuth to your unknown location. And that is where you must go. Intersection is looking at two known points like mountain tops and shooting an azimuth to find out where you are now.

Well, I was off to my new location to see what was next. The mountains were beautiful, to say the least. Not sure if I was in Alaska or where, but that was what

I assumed from the looks of things around me. I supposed the weapons were for killing bears and such, which would be great protein and warmth.

I started making my way toward the peak that I needed to cross. I figured by the map it was about five miles or halfway to the mark. I walked and walked, and it was very exhausting, to say the least. The altitude was killing me. I wasn't sure how high I was, but I had been working at sea level for some time. As you get higher, there is less oxygen, and you run out of air sooner. No problem, I thought. I will adjust in a week or so. I kept my pace and then realized there was no use killing myself; I needed to just slow down and do it right. I didn't want to lose my bearing or run out of water or use up too much nutrition.

I finally made it to the bottom of this gorgeous mountain and looked up thinking this was really going to suck. I filled up my water from a creek I found nearby and started my journey. It was a very slow process. I never thought the mountain had a top. To be honest, I kept climbing and climbing, wondering if I would ever make this peak. The snow was not easy to walk in. I kept sinking down and down. It was really taking a toll on me. I was not ready to climb these types of mountains. I wasn't in shape at all for this. However, I kept remembering there was no time limit. Take your time, stupid, I told myself.

So, I slowed down and took more time. I wanted to make it over the peak by nightfall, but I could see that I was running out of daylight. I needed to stop and hunker down for the night. I found a good place that still had a few trees and some cover. I scooped up snow to make a wind block and laid my poncho down and snuggled up in my poncho. It was cold, but I didn't need a fire right now. Of course, I was hot and sweaty, which is a big no-no in the mountains; that is how you get hyperthermia. So I sat there getting colder and thought, Hell with this; I need a little fire. Fire helps in so many ways. Fire will help you stay warm, keep predators away, and most of all, give you hope, a sense of security.

I gathered up little branches and began to build my fire. Also, the needles on the branches would make a nice bed in the snow. I gathered up just enough wood to build a fire for a few hours. After that it was all on me and the cold. I wished I could have found more, but beggars can't be choosy.

When the next morning came, I hadn't gotten a whole lot of sleep. Froze my ass off. That little poncho liner just didn't quite do it for me. It was time to head up the mountain and get some heat going into me. The sun was coming up and felt so good. Up and up I climbed. I was finally up to about the peak when I realized that this was not going to be an easy climb at all. It looked like I had to try and scale some steep rough rocks. I hadn't really seen that coming, but there was no turning back at this time.

I didn't have any climbing rope, and I should have tried to bypass this, but again, a little late for that. It only looked like about twenty feet of shit. I can do this, I told myself. I finally made it to the top of the peak. Damn, was I tired! The altitude was kicking my ass. I could hardly breathe; I just had no oxygen at this level. I needed to get my tail end off this peak and work my way down. I could also feel the headache coming in; I had to move down and get out of here. However, before I did, I had to shoot my compass heading and then make sure I was on the right track.

I headed down the mountain, finding it a lot easier going down the mountain than coming up it. I finally made my way down and sat down for a drink and protein bar. I was really trying not to eat them, but I had not come across anything else to eat yet. Not much to eat at twelve feet. Now that I was at the lower altitude, maybe I could find some veggies or something to shoot. If I could get an animal, that could last me awhile.

I looked at the map and realized I was about two miles from the point of interest. I was excited to see what was there. I was hoping for some food. But I knew that wasn't going to happen. Especially because this was a survival course. I made my way down and came to a flag and a box. Yay. I made the first contact on day two. I opened the box. Inside I found a grid coordinate to the next point of interest. Guess what, nothing else. This really sucked. I really wasn't expecting anything, but I had hoped for something else.

I checked out the map and as I was sitting by a stream. I figured they'd put me here so I could gather some water. I investigated the stream and saw some water crescents. This is like salad in the creek bed. Good, I can eat that, I thought. There are not many nutrients in there, but enough to fill me up.

BOB W. CANNADY

As I was reading my map, plotting my course, something caught my eye. I was sitting next to a big-ass bear track. Must be a grizzly, I thought. Two more thoughts entered my head. First: It would taste great. Second: Oh shit, that's a big bear. But where there is bear, maybe there is fish or berries to eat.

These thoughts started to make me hungry, and after the map deal, I was out scouting. I was so hungry I thought about eating part of my clothing. Ha-ha. Not that hungry yet, but I was getting there anyway. I put the coordinates in and looked at where I had to go. It appeared to be about twenty-two miles away. Holy shit, this was going to be a track through the mountains and very easy to get turned around. Now it was time to find something to eat. If the bears were here, that meant food somewhere. There wasn't much time, and I found some cranberries. They were a little sour to the taste but high in vitamin C and needed nutrients.

I studied the map, trying to find the best way to make this endless journey through the mountains. This was one hell of a long hike. I saw the mountain that I had on my map that I needed to get to, and I knew I didn't have to follow the course in a straight line. All I had to do was get to that mountain on the map and then look back, shoot my azimuth, and then get my back azimuth and keep on rolling. The mountain in the distance was a long, long way to go. I estimated on the map that it was around a ten-mile stretch, and it was going to take me all day, if not two days, to get there. Not an easy hike. Good thing that looking ahead I just had to make a walk to the mountain and then again use my compass once I got there. Easy peasy.

I filled up as many berries as I could grab and munched on them as I left. I figured there would be much more along the way. The mountains were breathtaking, to say the least. I'm from Montana, so this felt like home to me. This was my environment. I made it about four or five miles and figured I would find a good place to rest and just chill for the night. I was extremely tired and needed a good rest.

I came upon another small stream and figured this was as good a stopping place as any. I had lots of views in every direction and a nice place to sleep. I was low enough that the snow wasn't bad or too cold. Up on the mountain where I would have to cross, it looked horrible. Not sure how I was going to get up there and make that one.

I made my little area, and the sun was still out for a few, so I thought I could use the magnifying glass to start a fire. I got it started rather easily and began gathering dead wood. I figured I gathered enough to maybe stay warm tonight. I moseyed around looking for food or berries. Didn't find anything. I investigated the stream, hoping for a fish, but nothing, not even a little brook trout. It was OK; I still had my protein bars and berries. I figured one bar a day was enough to keep me going. I did need some kind of animal to eat. I was really hoping for a rabbit, but again nothing yet.

I decided not to use a lot of wood so that I could conserve more to burn at night when it was colder. I found myself falling asleep. I was exhausted from the altitude, and hiking was wearing me out faster than I'd thought it would. I wasn't in the best of shape and didn't expect this at all. No worries—I just listened to the noises and fell back asleep.

It was around 11:00 p.m. when I heard the noise of wolves. I knew now I was somewhere in Alaska. I had to be, given the mountains, wolves, and grizzly bears. I had to keep my wits about me and move on to the next location soon. I also knew that wolves are curious creatures, so if they saw the fire, they would surely pay me a visit.

I was sure glad they'd given me two guns at this point. Wolves never bothered me, though. You just must not be afraid and stand your ground and make noise so they think you are not easy prey. Wolves are predators, and if they think you are a bigger predator, then that can deter them. Also, if they sense you are scared, you have lost. You need to show no fear and be aggressive. I was not afraid of anything now. I considered them food. Besides, I had a rifle and pistol. That meant lots of food. This time walking I could really use some meat.

The night went on, and nothing exciting happened except I got some good rest. The sun was coming up, and I ate the last of the berries hoping that I would find something on the way to Mount Everest. I followed the creek up the mountain when the most wonderful item came into view. I found blueberries. OMG, they were so good! I ate them until I was about sick. I packed as much as I could with me and kept hiking on to the base of the mountain.

MONSTER

After a long and tiring walk, I finally made it to the base. By now it was getting late in the evening, and I was exhausted again. I needed to make a camp before making the climb. I was really not looking forward to this trek up the hill. Again, I made a small camp and gathered some wood. I wanted to use my magnifying glass so I could conserve my matches for emergencies.

I fell fast asleep and slept most of the night. I listened to the wolves howling, and out I went. The next morning was nice, still cold but nice. No wind, and everything was very calm. It was absolutely gorgeous. It was too bad I didn't have company with me to enjoy it. but that was OK; I'd spent many days by myself in the military, so solitude wasn't a big issue with me.

I thought how long I could possibly be out here; I figured a few weeks at best. I could do that on my head, I thought, as I walked up the mountain. The mountain was huge, and there were many different paths I could take, so I just walked cross path instead of straight up and down. Took a little longer but made the climb easier. After the whole day was about done and the sun was getting lower in the sky, I was about to reach the top. I was so happy and freezing my ass off. If I had to pee, I would have to squat. It was shriveled up. Ha-ha. I looked back at my old area and shot my azimuth. I had to move about two hundred yards on top of this mountain to get a good back azimuth. A back azimuth example is if you are going less than 180 degrees, then you add 180 to it. For example, I shot azimuth at 120, so I needed to add 180, and that would give me an angle of 300 degrees. Remember, there are only 360 degrees in a compass. So, if it is over 180, then you have to take away 180. For example, if I looked at my old camp and it was 220 degrees, I would subtract 180 degrees, and it would be 40 degrees.

So, I shot my angle after I moved across the top of the mountain and realized I was close to my original azimuth. I checked it out on the map and shot a resection to make sure I was at my point, and I was within a few degrees. I was good to go. I shot my heading and looked into the distance trying to find a good point of reference and start the track down.

I checked the map, and I still had about eight miles to go. I can do this, I thought. It's all downhill except for the flag marking my next objective. For some strange reason, it looked to be on the side of a mountain. Why would they put a flag on the mountain? I stopped trying to figure them out a long time ago. I made my way down the mountain and toward my objective. In the distance, I could see the mountain that looked to be the one with the flag and was hoping to make it there the following day. I wasn't sure how long this was going to take me. I was exhausted and hungry.

I kept on for several hours until the light began going away. I knew I needed to start a fire with the glass again, so I found a good place to shut down for the night. Tonight was cold, so cold that I shivered throughout the night. I woke up to another great morning, and off I went. I was very excited to see if there were any goodies in the box. I was hoping anyway.

MONSTER

I was about four hundred yards from the box and flag, and go figure: the contour curves were extremely close on the map. That meant it was steep as hell. It took me quite a while to get there, but I managed, and I found the flag and box. I remember just sitting there staring at it and praying that food was inside or something besides a grid coordinate.

I finally broke down and opened the box…fucking grid coordinate. Fuck, I was pissed. Nothing, nothing, nothing. They got me. I was depressed and tired of these damn coordinates and nothing else. I was exhausted and hungry, and this is what I got. FUCK!

I sat down and looked at the coordinate and put them on the map. I could see again I was about fifteen miles from the next objective. However, this time the track didn't quite look as bad. It appears that I didn't have to trek up some damn mountain, but I could follow some river for most of the way, which meant bears and fish. Either one, I didn't care. I needed to eat. I guessed this was why they put me here: so I could find some food. They must have known I would be hungry by now and need food. They were smarter than I was, and it was very planned out. OK, let's do this.

I made my way back down the mountain and called it quits. I was just tired and didn't feel like doing anything today. They told me no time limit, so fuck it, I thought. I'm resting the night and will start tomorrow.

The night came and went, and the next day I was ready to go. I was already feeling the effects of starvation and exhaustion. Not just that I was weary; I was very frustrated. I knew it was because of lack of sleep and food. Plus, I hated to admit it, but I was tired of being by myself too. Not sure why, but I was. It sure would have been nice to have someone going through misery like I was. Do you call that selfish? I often wondered why they were putting me through this kind of training. I went through this in the military, and they knew it. Why again?

I am sure they have their reasons, I thought, and if I want to be part of their big picture, I have to do what I am told like a good soldier. Ahhhhhhh. So, I moved on to the next objective and found myself lost in my own thoughts looking at the beauty of Alaska. The mountains were just gorgeous with snow on them and so was the valley full of green grass and flowing water.

I made it down to a river, and when I say river, I meant a big-ass river. By the looks of the map, I would have to cross this damn thing sooner or later. I was not happy about being wet, but I knew they had to do that to test me swimming and freezing. That was just the way they are. I found a nice little place under a big rock for cover. I thought I had gone far enough by now, and this would be a great place to look for fish and have a nice fire.

I gathered up some wood and went out fishing. Well, not fishing with a pole but trying to find a fish I could get with my hands if that was possible. I had done this many times in a stream but not a river. Plus, I thought I might run into a bear or something. I didn't care. I was hungry and cold, and I knew I had to cross this river eventually.

I thought about crossing and getting that over with, but the current seemed rather fast and furious. Even though I was a great swimmer and could make it, I would rather find a better spot. I was up the river about a hundred yards when fuck me—I saw a small black bear on the other side. You simply have no idea what that did to my self-esteem. It was time to eat. Although he was on the other side, it didn't matter, I was going to kill him and swim for it. If I had to camp for a few days, then that is what I would do.

I had shot bears before in Montana, so this was nothing for me. However, I didn't really like killing animals, but this was survival, and I was starving. So, I raised the rifle and shot him dead. I was so happy. However, all the wood I'd gathered was now wasted; I had to get across the river for dinner.

I walked up farther, trying to find somewhere in the river with less debris and maybe a nice big turn or a fork. When a river forks, that is less water, which can make it more accessible. Always look for the widest part, too, and the deepest. It is usually less swift. The best method to cross a river like this is to put your feet downriver and float on your back while trying to swim at an angle. It takes a little while but is safer.

I made it up maybe three hundred yards from the bear and knew I could make it over to him by then. I wasn't sure what was below and didn't want to take a chance on some waterfall or something. So, I waded in and went for a Hail Mary. The current was very strong, and I was being sucked down quickly. I swam for dear life, trying to make my way to the other side. The water was ice cold and had no mercy on my dumbass.

I saw trees floating down the river and prayed I wouldn't be hit by one. This was extremely difficult trying to swim with my head facing upriver and feet facing down. The river kept turning me around and flipping me this way and that. The river was very unforgiving and probably not the best place to cross. It was also difficult carrying a pack and rifle. I don't have any idea how much water I took into my mouth, but it was gallons, or so it felt.

The worst thing was my energy level was significantly low. I had not eaten much and was very low on energy. However, what makes you different from the rest is your drive to survive. Too many people would just give up. This is nothing, I kept telling myself. It's just a damn river, get to the other side. I kept swimming and swimming like my life depended on it. Oh, yeah, it fucking did.

I saw the bear as I passed it by and was almost to shore. Maybe ten feet away. I kicked and clawed to get there, and finally after a few more yards, I was home sweet home. When I say I was tired that was not even close to how I felt. I was mentally and physically exhausted. I drug my ass up on the shore and just lay there like a fat pig. Couldn't believe how out of shape I was. I was not expecting all of this. However, dinner was soon to be served.

I made my way back to the bear and started gathering wood. The first thing I did was skin him. I was going to use this hide for warmth. After I skinned the little bear, I began to cut off meat. Then I planted two Y-shaped sticks on either side of the fire. I cut a pointed end on a bigger stick and slid some meat on it. I rested the big stick across the fire on the upright sticks. I kept on cutting meat off the bear. I was going to have meat for a while. I then stripped down and put my clothes near the fire to try and dry everything out. I was in heaven but cold as shit. I needed clothes and my Woobie.

After about an hour or so, the meat was done, and I pulled it off. I then put more meat on the stick and started cooking so that this bear's life was not to be wasted. I cooked as much as I could carry. After getting dressed I started scraping the bear's hide to take off the fat. I needed the hide for warmth, even though it was not very light. I put my knife by the fire to get it nice and hot. This would help with taking the fat off the hide while also searing it the best I could with the time I had.

I laid the hide down and began eating and scraping again. This wasn't a big bear, maybe two years old. I scraped and scraped until most of it was off. I put it in the river a few times to help get it cleaned and so forth. Again, trying to tan a hide is very time consuming, and I didn't have the time to do it properly, and this would have to suffice. I worked on it for some time and then just sat around and ate.

In the meantime, I had dug a hole by the river about three feet away to let the water soak in so I could have somewhat clean water that was filtered by the earth. Plus, I didn't want to get the shits out here or stomach issues. So I tried to be careful.

It was getting close to nightfall, and I was stuffed to my gills with bear. I kept wondering if this smell would bring in bigger bears. I was a little worried about that, but my gut took over and I needed to eat, or I was done. I had no choice but to do what I had to do. Again, sorry for the kill, but it was truly a survival situation for me.

I stayed there for a few days to just recuperate. After the next few days, I was acclimated to the climate and full of protein and warmth. I was ready to go. I knew if I followed the river, I was bound to find other bears in the area and frankly surprised nothing had come around me for the last few days. I was just mentally drained and needed a good break. Now I was ready to attack anything that they threw at me. Again, they had known I would find a bear down here to eat. That was why they never gave me any food in the box. They knew exactly what they were doing. Of course, I am sure I wasn't the first one that ever did this course. I just wondered how many had made it this far. I had been gone for days on very little, and the weather was very cold in the mountains. It was just cold.

I had checked the map, and I was about three miles from my next point, which was fine. I often wondered if this was it or was there more. I really was enjoying myself on this adventure but was getting a little tired of it. It sure would have been nice to have been out here with a team or someone. But again, they did this for some reason. I guessed I just had to trust them.

I made it to the next point and saw the flag and box. I wasn't really excited to see the box. I knew what was in it: a fucking coordinate. I opened the box and yes, a coordinate, nothing else. *Whaaaaaaaaat a fuckinngg surprise!*

I took it out and plotted it on my map. And what a nice surprise: another fucking twenty miles of shit. I was pissed to say the least. Damn it anyway. Oh well, time to go. I saw I could follow the river for a few miles before veering off. So, I made my way down and then looked at what I had to go through. I was not impressed. I was heading back up the mountains and crossing peaks again. This time it did not look like fun at all. This was miserable, and now I was carrying this hide with me. I just thought to myself, It never ends. Why are they doing this? I already showed them I could find points and use a map. What are they looking for? I missed my boys and was just lonely, I guess. Was this my life? What was I doing? I guess at this point, being so far away and going back to the mountains had its toll on me. I was just depressed and pissed.

I made it for a while and had no energy. I guess the mind thing was messing with me. They knew just what they were doing, fuckers. This was a major head fucking. Now the question was: Let them win or me win? I couldn't quit—it wasn't in me—but I can tell you I was tired of this shit already and the mountains I was about to face really pissed me off.

I started up the small hill, looking around so I could get a clear scope of the terrain and get a good azimuth to the next site. I finally made it to the top, and just like the map showed, there were a whole bunch of fucking mountains to climb. Damn it, I was pissed. But I just took my time and moved on. I swear if the next point is like this, I told myself, I am kicking their ass when I see them.

I was at the top of this little mountain, and as I looked down in this valley, I could see a big, beautiful field and a big-ass grizzly. Right where I must go. I thought about it, and this was the perfect place to go but I really didn't want to mess with the bear right now. I just wanted to bypass him and cause no trouble for either one of us. So I picked another path that was not so nice and started off.

Damn grizzly, I wanted to just shoot him for making me do this crap. I tracked up the hill and made my way around big and stupid. I walked and walked, but weird to say, I was getting into better shape and wasn't dying so much now. I was moving better. By the time I got around him, I was near the base of the hill. I could see the v that I had to get to. But it was nighttime, and I was again tired and exhausted.

I didn't sleep very well thinking of big and stupid coming up on me and eating me for dinner. Nothing happened, and I was fine. So I gathered up my things and took a nice healthy crap for the first really long time. Man, that was great. But I think all the meat had stuffed me up because it was like shitting out two kids. I tore my butt up, and no, there was no toilet paper, just some water to clean myself with.

I looked up at the mountain, and it wasn't as bad as the other two. I just took my time and made it before nightfall. Of course, my thinking I was in good shape slapped me around a bit because it did kick my ass a little. I again shot my azimuth and went down this mountain to see nothing but other mountains in front of me. I went to find a place to camp.

MONSTER

The next day I saw I had to go through a valley and was relieved to get a little rest from climbing. I made my way down there. Now this is going to be hard to believe, but I saw a small cabin out in the middle of bum fuck Egypt. I had to investigate. I could see an antenna on it, and it looked uninhabited. I pushed the door open, and lo and behold, it was one of their cabins. How did they fucking know I would find this? I guess the only way to the next point was these directions. So once again they knew more than I did. I went into this little piece-of-shit cabin with a small stove and lots of MREs (Military Meals Ready to Eat). I was grateful for that. There was a radio with a note. It said: *Turn on every morning at 0930. Wait 5 minutes; if you don't hear anyone, turn it off and continue until you are reached. Also, the food you have here can make it if you conserve your rations.*

I looked at the food, and there were fifteen meals. What does that mean? One per day? Half per day? How long was I supposed to be here? I was not happy, and of course, no bed or anything but a small stove with matches. How fucking nice of them.

Well, at least I wasn't hiking anymore for a while. That was the bright side to this. I figured I would eat half an MRE a day just in case I was here a month or whatever.

I made myself a little bed with my poncho and pack for a pillow and sat in there. Let me tell you, I think this was the hardest part of the whole adventure. Day after day I sat in there and turned on the radio to hear nothing but static. I was about to lose my fucking mind. I had cabin fever times ten.

It had been five days and still nothing. I kept going outside to not lose my mind. This was a tough one. When are they going to answer the radio and tell me to get out of here?

On the eighth day, I was miserable as can be. I thought they really forgot about me and wanted to go to the next point. I was literally tired of talking to myself in this fucking cabin! The next day came, and I turned on the radio, and to my surprise someone was there. The only thing he said was, "Move to your next location; leave all remaining food there." And hung up. Damn it, damn it, damn it. What does that mean I can't take any with me? Can I gorge myself? I was hungry and starving myself. Gosh damn it! I knew I couldn't eat anymore and couldn't sneak any out. Damn fucking bastards. I was losing my ever-loving mind.

I grabbed my pack and left this godforsaken place. I was really pissed I hadn't eaten more. I shot my compass and started off. Fuck, I was pissed! I knew I had a big mountain to climb and was still fucking far away from the next point. I was really in a shitty mood now. Never in my life had anything been this hard. I guess just not knowing anything and this fucking cabin shit killed my spirit. I was a mess and pissed, but what do you do? Keep trucking on, I guess.

Needless to say, it took me a good part of two and half days to make it to the next point, and I swore if there was another coordinate in there, I was going to flip the fuck out. I saw the flag a few hundred yards away in a nice clearing, and this was nice. I walked over to the box and stood there looking like a dumbass waiting for a miracle. I knew what was in it. I was just beaten down.

I opened the box, and a note told me to push the button that I had been carrying around. It also told me I was not allowed to speak to anyone that I came in contact with. I had to just shut up and not say anything. What the hell did that mean?!

I sat there for about an hour when a helicopter landed. I went over to it and climbed in. No surprise here. Needle in my arm, and out I went.

Chapter 5

TEST 3B FINAL: NAVIGATIONS/ SURVIVAL (ISOLATION DESERT)

FUCKKKKKKKKKKKKKKKKKKKKKKKKKKK KK!!!!!!!!!!!!!!!!!!!!!!!!!!!!!!

I just woke up in the fucking desert! With the fucking can next to me and my pack! What the hell just happened? I can't believe I am in the desert. It appears they just drugged me out and dumped me off. No nothing. Not a hi or goodbye, nothing but a needle and a wake-up to hot-ass desert. Not a happy person right now. I should have figured as much. I thought my test was done. It appears not!

I stood up and just kicked the can and yelled in the sky, like the idiot that I am. Well, I guess the test isn't over; I have desert training to do. What the hell am I up against now? Time to look and see what I have.

I opened the can up, and wow, what a fucking surprise: a fucking grid coordinate. I really hate these guys. I looked over to see my pack full, so I dug in and saw there were no weapons. That is just great, not a gun of any sort, I thought. I guess out here there isn't much to use one on.

Pack items were

1. One hundred feet of paracord
2. Magnifying glass
3. Poncho
4. Woobie
5. Big-ass knife
6. Canteen cup
7. Box of matches
8. Fifteen protein bars
9. Full camelback water pouch
10. A gallon water jug
11. Hat
12. Sunglasses
13. *No* fucking toilet paper (and I have to shit!)
14. Map with a marker
15. *No* damn compass (fuck!)

The compass thing really pissed me off. It is hard enough to navigate with a compass, but without, I would have to use the damn stupid-ass stars and sun. *Shiiiitiitiiitit!*

I see the point is about five miles away, so this shouldn't be too bad, I hope. Please make the point easy to see. I had everything marked on the map and knew I had a straight shot north, so they were trying to make it somewhat easy to start out, I thought. Who the hell knew with these assholes.

I had an idea from the sun as to which way to go but thought I would take a little time and use the stick method to make sure I had a good heading. The stick method is very simple. Stick a stick in the ground so it casts a shadow on the ground and place a rock over the end of the shadow. Then wait for twenty minutes while the shadow moves and place another rock over the end of the shadow. Stand on the two rocks with your back facing the stick, and you are facing north.

So off I went on my new mission and journey to see what was in store for me. After walking a mile or so, I came across some small trees and branches. I found one that would make a great stabbing stick if I came across a snake or something, so I sharpened it up and started walking with it. Don't forget the gallon of water; that was just great. I got to lug that thing around too. Not like I wanted to, but it would be great water holder if I found some *fucking* water out here.

I knew desert survival, so I just needed to calm the fuck down and get after it. Two big things to look for are birds and insects. They tend to lead you to water. Of course, canyons and green vegetation. I was just glad that the three topographical maps were with me. I could see the canyons ahead and knew I was going in the right direction. I was just not a happy camper at this moment. Also, I needed to find a place out of the sun for now and conserve my water and travel at night using the stars better. Walking at night in the desert is the best way to travel. However, when I was getting close to the target, I would need to move in the daylight so I could see the damn flag and stupid-ass can.

After about two miles, I made it to the canyons and knew I had about three miles left. Again, I was tired from the drugs and hot; the best thing for me now would be to wander around in the canyon not losing direction, seek a cool place to sleep, and possibly find food and water. I should have known these assholes would put me in the desert just to torture my ass. I should have known.

As I made my way around the canyons, I was walking through tunnels that were carved out by water some thousands of years ago. I have to say they were beautiful to walk through and actually quite cool. However, they had no signs of life or water. Of course not; it was the fucking desert. Not even a nasty-ass cesspool. But I was fine as of now. I just needed to get as close to the point of interest and bed down till dark.

After about an hour I found an opening, and I could go out and see where the hell I was. So I climbed up and looked around. By the map I was within a few miles of the point. So I decided to shoot another angle at north using sticks I had put in my pack to help me along. After that I used some rocks to make an arrow pointing in the direction I needed to go and crawled back down to bed for the day.

I knew I could easily make it to the point right now, but I didn't want to use my water up in the day. I really needed to conserve because I just didn't know what I was going up against and needed to be safe. Oh yes, I forgot; I did have the button in case I needed help.

I lay down in the cool sand in the shade under the rocks. I put my pack down and crashed out. I must have been tired because I woke up in the dark. Well, it was time to roll, I guessed, and get to my coordinate and the shit can and find the next point. I really hated that can.

I made my way up to the rocks I had laid out, saw my point of direction, and headed out. I hadn't drunk much water because again I didn't want to have to drink my own piss to survive. But knowing these assholes, that was coming. I walked the usual number of steps to make a mile: approximately 1,983 for me. How I kept track of how far I walked was simple. I had a long strand of rope on my shoulder that came down to about my waist. Every time I took one hundred steps, I would tie a small knot to indicate that I'd gone one-tenth of a mile. After ten knots, I'd walked one mile. My little paracord rope had enough for three miles approximately. It was enough to keep me on track. I had approximately two knots to go, and I should find the can. I was hoping anyway.

Counting steps was an old military trick. However time-consuming, it was a great way to keep track of distance especially if you didn't have a map. But this was a topographical map, so life was simple. I kept on tying my knots and moving through the desert. At this time, I could see really nothing of mountains and such. I could see a few small ones, but that was about it. Again, I was hoping not to step on a snake and get shut down. I walked very slowly and cautiously.

Time went on and I could see that I was getting close to the point, and by the looks of things, I should be able to see the marker. It was mostly flat with little sand dunes. The moon was shining brightly, and the night was gorgeous. I walked and walked in the cool air, still pissed about having to go through this again. My temperament was slowly losing hostility, though, and I was back in the mood to navigate.

I made it to the fucking can and flag. How I thought about taking a nice crap in the can, but I held that off for now. I figured after the end of this, I would be back to being pissed and would then do it. But for now, all I could do was stare at the can and wonder if by some miracle something besides a grid coordinate was inside. Like a fucking candy bar and Coke.

I reached over and opened the can. What a fucking surprise! Just a piece of shitty paper with a point on it. Aaaaaaaaaaaaaaaaahhhhhhhhhhhhhhhhhhhh! I really hate these people, I thought. I pulled out the map and plotted my next course. This time it had me going north again. Why are they leading me straight north and not east or west? I wondered. What the hell are they up to? Why didn't they just keep me going farther? Maybe because of the heat? I had no idea, but the next coordinate was approximately ten miles away. Not bad because at night, I could make that rather easily before morning.

I started off using the Big Dipper bucket pointing at Polaris, and off I went. It's a little trickier at night. Another easy way to navigate is to put two sticks in the ground, imagine there is a line tied to the top of them, and look at a star in the direction you want to go and keep following it. Look for a bright star, even Polaris. It makes life even simpler in keeping with a straight line.

I undid the knots in my step-counting rope and went on my merry way. The stars were really beautiful that night, and I could see the stars that I wanted to follow quite easily. I was just praying that cloud cover didn't come into play; then I would be screwed for a day. But nonetheless I was moving along and again slowly because of snakes and cactus.

I could see blurbs of rocks on the ground and nothing too exciting. I had traveled about two miles when I saw something in the distance. It looked like trees or something; I couldn't really make it out. However, they were off to my west side, and I really didn't want to detour much. However, trees meant water, I hoped. Ah, what the hell—a little detour.

Now deviating from your route at night can be difficult because it can throw you off your flag and traveling straight. I had stopped to look at the map as best I could. I was hoping for a Popsicle stand on the map. Just my luck: there was nothing on the map that showed a pond or anything. So this was how I was going to do it without getting off track too much.

I walked until I was directly west of my position and probably around three hundred yards or so away. This wasn't too bad, but also remember things in the dark can be deceiving. It might have been one mile or even farther. So my first task was to put my stick on the ground and tie a piece of clothing to it. I used the top part of my sock; this I could see and would probably need in the future. This would help me get back to the stick and keep on my path better. I then put rocks down in an arrow facing the way that I was walking to the north. Now I just did a left turn and started walking straight to the trees. I also made knots on the bottom of my string so I would not mess up my count to the other point.

After about two hundred yards or so, I came to the shitty-ass trees, or should I say sticks. I looked around a bit to see if the ground was possibly wet. I could see an old creek bottom, so thought I would double-check and dig down about a foot or so. If I felt anything moist, then I would go farther. As usual, nothing but dry dirt. I needed to get back to the stick and sock. The last thing I wanted to do was get caught out in the heat with no cover. I would surely die of dehydration.

After about an hour of screwing around digging around, I made it back to the stick. I picked it up and looked at my point of direction and headed out. The bad thing was I needed to pee. So I did what I had to do. I peed in my hands as slowly as I could and wiped it on my head and neck to try and cool me down. The water from the pee will help keep you cool in the air or wind. So yes, I have stunk like piss.

I walked a total of six miles and realized that in a few more hours it would be daylight. This bothered me some. I could see no visual signs of cover. However, I did have my poncho with me to make a tent, if possible, to just keep me out of the sun. I put my sticks back in the ground and checked out my star, and I was on track. I thought maybe they would not keep me in the middle of the fucking desert to die and at least lead me to cover or water. But who was I kidding? They wanted me miserable. I had the button if it got too bad. The desert is definitely one of the worst environments to live in.

I was within about one mile now of the point. Still no cover! No nothing, really. I just kept tracking on with only a few hours left. After another thirty minutes, I was in the area of the can and the stake. But to my surprise, there was nothing I could see. This now really bothered me. How did I screw this up? I thought. No way I could make it back and start over. It had to be here somewhere. I just couldn't see anything. I remained calm and didn't panic. Of course, lots of swear words came out and out and out.

I thought, "What the hell!" Ten miles for me navigating by the stars was a stretch. I could navigate, but I was no Magellan. I sat there looking in all directions and couldn't see anything. OK, think, I told myself. I know I reached three miles and untied the string, and three more miles and untied the string, and three more miles and untied the string, and I should have ten knots now. I counted, and I was at ten knots. I was in the area, but again I was not walking on pavement; I was walking on sand. What does sand do to your steps? I asked myself. It makes them shorter.

This meant the stake should be farther ahead. I unraveled my knots to start over and walk a bit longer, maybe two or three hundred yards at best. I stacked three rocks that were about six inches in diameter on top of each other so I could come back to the spot if needed. I started off in the northern direction and kept a strong lookout. I figured if I didn't find anything soon, I was going to wait till daylight and look then and maybe do a circle navigation around my stick. The stars were gone, and daylight was coming. I should be able to see the damn stick soon.

I was at the three-hundred-yard mark and didn't see anything. I can honestly say I was a little worried now. I could have missed my mark by hundreds of yards. Damn it. I found a big rock and just sat there for a minute waiting for the sun. I had to find this son of a bitch, or I was in trouble. I kept beating myself up over missing the flag. Just don't know how I did. I couldn't be that far off.

The sun was up, and I could feel the warmth coming in. Now I should be able to find it. I had about half a gallon left and half a camelback full of water, and this would go quick in the heat. I was not feeling good about this at all. I checked out the map and could see some points of interest and where the point should have been. Unfortunately, without a compass it really made it more difficult.

I studied the map as best I could and couldn't see anything like a landmark. The terrain just looked the same as where I was. I saw a hill several miles away and looked at the contours on the map, trying to get a direction to it so I could find the point. I finally came up with the idea that I was maybe a few hundred yards west. Remember, if your right dominates you, your right leg is stronger and you will never walk in a straight line; you will eventually curve to the left. Maybe this was it.

I knew the rock I was sitting on, so I just headed west. I had tied knots on the bottom of my string for about 350 yards when I thought I saw the can about 200 yards to my south. That could make sense. I walked in that direction, and lo and behold, the flag was flying and the fucking can was there. You could have felt my heart aching in excitement.

I went over and thought, I need to get out of this sun. Please be water and let me roll out of here. Fuck nooooo! Coordinate!

I hurried and plotted the coordinate down and double-checked it. It looked like I needed to go north again for four miles. OK, I can do this. Navigating during the day is much easier for me, so I was off. I had to make up some time and try and find shelter somewhere on the way. I was walking almost at a steady pace thinking they surely wouldn't leave me out here with no chance of finding water or giving me some, would they?

I could see something ahead of me about thirty minutes into this hike. It looked like trees or some kind of brush. Whatever it was, that is where I was going to stay and get out of this heat. I made it to the brush, and it looked a little green. I was about three hundred yards from a rocky hill in front of me. If I stayed here, I could use the brush to hang my poncho up and get out of the heat. If I made it to the point, maybe there was water. I gave it a fifty-fifty chance. I took the brush.

I hung up my poncho and got out of the sun. The cover made it bearable to rest. I lay down and tried to get shut-eye. This was very difficult because of the heat. But once again the pee came into play and cooled me down. But of course, the creek bed kept calling me to go dig in it. The brush was a little bit green; maybe, just maybe, something was under there.

I dug about a foot and half and didn't even really feel any moisture. This was not good. I would be out of water soon. I really needed to find something. So I just hunkered down and had a bite and slept as best I could.

I woke up, and it was still daylight but getting dusk. I noticed a damn scorpion on the ground and thought, I have wood and sticks; time to eat. I did need some protein but didn't really want to eat it because it would make me thirsty. But what the hell. If there was one, maybe I could get more. I stuck him with my knife and cut off his stinger. If you cook them on a stick, you can eat them whole. Legs and shell—everything.

I put him down and then looked under some rocks and found two more. That was enough; time to cook. I made a little twig fire—just enough to cook them and eat, then leave. I can tell you this: they were good, and I was ready to go see what lay ahead.

I made it to the next rocky outpoint and had just a little way to find the stake. So I kept on walking, and then I came across my water source. It was the nastiest piece of shit water I had ever seen. But it was water, and I needed to clear it up and drink. I filled up my camelback with the remaining water and also filled up my canteen cup. I needed to make a fire now. But unfortunately, I didn't have any wood. So, yes, I tracked back to the brush and loaded it up so I could boil lots of the cesspool and fill up my gallon jug. It was the best plan of action, and hell with the flag right now; I needed supplies.

I made it back and started in by boiling the water and cooling it for a minute before putting it in my jug. I had to fill it all the way and kept doing this over and over until I was full and ready. In fact, this was a good place to just hide out for a day. I had cover and could sit here for a while. The stake had to be about half a mile ahead, but I didn't even care. I needed this water to get fully hydrated before I started.

After several hours and going back to the brush, I was fully hydrated, and the jug was full. It was now daytime, and I thought to myself, I could sneak away and check out the stake and then come back if needed. I guess the curiosity got to me. The heat of the day was here, and against all my good judgment, I left.

I made it to the can and flag. Not hard this time. I opened up the box and found one fucking Oreo! Hey, I know what you are thinking: It's an Oreo, greedy bastard. I really wanted to eat it, but I thought I could use the sugar boost on the next hike out. I checked out the next grid coordinate, and it was leading me east this time. OK, I thought, it's in a different direction. This time I had about eight miles to go. I decided to go back to the rock and seek some cover and wait till night. However, I shot my azimuth with the sticks and put the rocks in an arrow again, just to get me going in the right direction and match them up with the North Star.

At dusk I headed out. I made great time and ate my Oreo on the way. I can tell you this it was better than any sex I'd ever had. Yum-yum. I was in heaven, and I savored every little bite. Not sure why they were so kind, but I really was appreciative of the cookie.

I looked at the map. I was about three hours into the track and saw that I was coming to some obstacles in the way. When I say obstacles, I mean hills. I didn't really look forward to this. I kept thinking about snakes and all kinds of crap crawling around on them. Plus, the hardest thing was to keep on track with my course. But I just kept on the course and hoped to get to the flag before the mountains. The mountains would take a toll on my water supply and my lack of energy.

I had almost made it to the mountains when I finally reached my steps and eight miles. Now I just needed to find the flag. Again, nowhere in sight. It was nearly dawn again, and I was really exhausted. I just called it quits and went over to the side of the mountain and figured I would find the flag later in the daylight. I was tired and worn out. Mountains were something I really didn't want to mess with right now. I found a small cave, kind of. Anyway, it would keep me out of the sun, and I wanted some shut-eye. Out I went.

I woke up with the sun still shining, not sure what time it was, but it looked like I had been out for quite a while. *It would have been nice to have a watch, assholes!*

I figured it was around four in the afternoon and still hot but not as bad. I got myself up and ate a protein bar and went out looking for the flag. Thank you, God, I could see it at the corner of the mountain. After looking at the map, it was plain to see. I guess I was somewhat delirious from having diarrhea all day and being a little dehydrated. I just hadn't seen it.

I walked over to the fucking can and opened it up. No cookie, no water, but a small note. Hmm, what is this? I thought. Of course, there were two coordinates on this one. The note that followed said: *Use your instincts and pick your next coordinate.* What did that even mean? My next coordinates? I wanted to go home, and that coordinate wasn't even on here. I plotted both of them and looked at them closely. One was going up the fucking mountain and over crap hills for six miles. That did not look good at all. The other looked to be walking on flat land and in the desert, but it was a much easier walk. But this one was around nine miles.

I sat there and thought about this for a while. Them bastards wanted me to take the easy route. They knew that was what most people would do because of less terrain and less obstacles. But it seemed weird to me. I knew if I trekked up the mountain, I would burn through my water supply and food intake. There was probably no water on these mountains, and water would surely be down low.

Use your instincts? My instincts were telling me to take the easy route. However, in a combat situation, never take a path. They will surely be watched or booby-trapped. My instincts kept telling me to go up the mountain. *Damn it, fucking no good bastards. Cocksuckers.* I shot my azimuth with sticks and looked in the distance and could see a peak I needed to get to. I was not sure how far, but on the map, it looked to be around four to five miles, depending on the hike. *Fucking assholes.* Now I was pissed off again and felt a surge of adrenaline shoot through me.

Up the damn mountain I went. I kept the peak in my sight and knew where I started from, so I had a clear line of sight for a while. I drank water like horribly. I couldn't stop drinking; I was dying inside. I felt really lightheaded and sick. I guess I was dehydrated from the shit water I had been drinking. I felt the need to pee. Yes, what do I do? I wondered. Drink it or use it to cool me down? I had a little water left in my jug and some in my camelback. What to do? I really hated these people. I poured my remaining water into the camelback and peed into the jug, just in case.

I kept walking and was really exhausted. I had a raging headache from lack of water and just wasn't sure I was going to make it. My steps were getting shorter and shorter step by step. I was out of breath and totally exhausted. I actually thought about pushing the button. I was getting delirious. But I only had a small way to go for the peak.

After another hour or so, I made the peak and realized I was about a mile from the point. It was almost daylight, and I didn't see anywhere to bed down. I had to keep going to the point and either die or find it. I was not doing well. By this time, I was out of water. I still had a few pee stops in my jug. I really didn't want to do this. I had to do it before, but this was hot and piss. I figured I would just puke doing it and cause myself more issues. I was almost done.

I went over to the next little corner and OMG! I saw the most beautiful sight in the world, a small running creek. I ran down the mountain and jumped in. Next I did the most horrible, unthinkable thing. I just drank the water. No purification, nothing. I just couldn't help myself. Not sure why I did this; I knew better, but I had to. I don't know if I could have waited. The best thing to do again was dig a hole next to the creek and let the water filter through the earth to it and then drink. I couldn't wait and didn't care.

After I lay in the water for a while, I crawled out and lay down on the ground. I saw green bushes, and everything looked great. I was in paradise or maybe dead—I wasn't sure at that point—but I didn't care either way. I just lay there for a long time. I was so exhausted.

I finally got up and started looking for the flag. I found it rather soon. I opened the box and found an MRE. I couldn't believe my eyes. I opened the MRE up and started in; I was literally starving to death. I only ate one thing out of there and figured I would save the rest. I looked in and saw the note. I opened it up, and you guessed it: coordinate. This time I was going to stay here for a few days and get myself in order before I went out. I was in bad shape and needed to heal myself.

I built me a little cover with my poncho. Pulled out my Woobie and lay down. I eventually got up and went off to the creek, dug my hole, and watched the water slowly trickle in. I decided I had time; I was going to boil everything and make sure I didn't get sick again. I guess I didn't boil the last batch enough.

I took my time and gathered some twigs for a fire and just relaxed. It felt so good. I loved these guys. I told them over and over, "Thank you for this." Then I realized they did this to me. Why the hell was I giving them credit for saving my life? Fucking brainwashing bastards.

I foraged for the next few days and found scorpions and one small snake. I ate them all. I drank as much as I could and waited to see if I was going to get sick or not. But all was good, and I was fully recovered. It was time now to look at leaving. My mental state was good. I had some food in me, and I could make the next track.

I studied the next point of interest, and this one was going to hurt. It was fifteen miles away and looked to be in desolate territory. I didn't see a lot of mountains but a few more landmarks, which is good for keeping track of where you are. The only issue on this trek was that it was to the northeast. Not a straight shot but in the middle. This would be a little trickier. But I was ready for this one. My feet were kind of healed up, my socks were dry, my clothes were clean, and so was I.

It was still daytime, and I had already shot my directions and was ready. I assumed it was about 4:00 p.m. again, time to head out. I was making good time and figured if I kept my pace up, I could easily make fifteen miles if I didn't have anything in the way. I humped and humped and was knocking it out.

About four hours into the hike, I came across another stream. Hey, this is great, I thought. I was just going to bed down here for the night and get more water and rehydrate my pack and jug and go tomorrow. Why not? It was evident that I had no time limit. So I could take my time and finish the mission and go home. I could not wait to see the boys and eat a steak. All I thought about was food. It is amazing when you have no food how much you cherish it when you do. I was hungry again and was trying to spare my crackers. That was all I had left. I needed the nutrients to make it.

I bedded down and boiled water and took another bath and just enjoyed the scenery. Imagine looking up at water-cut rocks from long ago and wondering how many people have been here before you. It was truly breathtaking, and I loved not dying of water. I was enjoying this but knew it would come to a stop soon.

The next day I shot my azimuth and lay around for a while until around 4:00 p.m. again. Best time to hike. I started off knowing I only had three or four hours of walking ahead of me. Not bad.

You got to be fucking kidding me! In the middle of nowhere, I found a fucking small-ass cabin. *Nnnnnnnnnnnnnnnonnnnnnnnnnnnnoooooooooo!* I really couldn't believe this shit again. Well, that was my point, and it was in the right spot. Damn it to hell. I knew what this meant. In the middle of the desert, no stream, no nothing, and just a stupid-ass cabin with antenna.

I walked in and saw the radio, six MREs and a ten-gallon water tank with a pump on top of it. Of course, the fucking dreaded letter. Here we go again. I stood there in disbelief and did not really want to open it. I was worn out and tired. I knew what it was going to say anyway. I was really getting tired and more tired of just being by myself. I didn't mind isolation, but this was wearing on my nerves.

I opened the letter, and it stated the following: *Turn on the radio at 3:00 p.m. for five minutes a day until you receive your next instructions.* That was it. I looked at the MREs and figured, OK, last time I didn't eat enough and saved too much food. They gave me six MREs, so I can eat half a day and last twelve days without starving myself too much. This way I will have energy to make it through just in case I am here longer than expected. I was really thinking maybe a week at most.

So I took them all out and separated them the best I could to ration for twelve days, yet enough to keep me healthy. I then filled my camelback up with water and drank a little to test it. All good. Next I used a little to fill up my jug just in case they told me to leave the food and water behind. I was making sure this time I was more prepared.

After all the stuff was ready for the week, I used my boot to clear out the sand the best I could and make a small little area for me to sleep in. I laid my poncho down and put some rocks on the corners to keep it nice and tight. I put my Woobie down and put my pack as my pillow. So now I would just wait, praying they would call after a few days and just let me rest. Although it was hot as hell out there, it was somewhat cooler inside out of the sun. I was ready!

Day One: Sat around thinking and just lying there, trying to conserve my water and food. Just wondering how long they were going to keep me here. I was tired of starvation, dehydration, and loneliness. I just wanted to go home and couldn't wait to be picked up soon by the helicopter on the next point. I went outside so I didn't get cabin fever and played around a little and just looked and wished I was at the stream instead of this spot. Nothing at 3:00 p.m.

Day Two: Same ole same ole. Sat around and waited. Nothing at 3:00 p.m.

Day Three: Sat around and waited. Starting to get really annoyed. Nothing at 3:00 p.m.

Day Four: Sat around and waited. Really getting annoyed. Nothing at 3:00 p.m.

Day Five: About to lose my shit. Really getting fucking annoyed. Tired of taking a crap and peeing in my hand to wipe my ass. I stink! No damn toilet paper because they took it out of the MREs. *Assholes!* Nothing at 3:00 p.m.

Day Six: Getting depressed wondering if they forgot me. Today I binge ate. I guess it was the depression and just being fucking hungry. Again wiping my ass with pee.

Damn MREs were making me shit too much. Nothing at 3:00 p.m.

Day Seven: They better fucking answer! I told myself. I have had it in this hot shithole. I want to leave and at least go to the next spot and get picked up. Really tired of this crap. I found myself talking a lot to myself and cussing them immensely. FUCKING nothing at 3:00 p.m.

Day Eight: Ahhhhhhhhhhhhhhh! Where in hell were they! I was just out of steam and wanted to move on so I could get home. I was fucking going stir crazy in this cabin. I needed to get out of here. Nothing, nothing, fucking nothing at 3:00 p.m.

Day Nine: OK, I told myself. Calm down, and today is the day. I was starting to get really low on food because of my fat-ass eating. I was down to two days of food and maybe they knew this. I would not starve, but fucking out is out! Aaaaaahhhhhhhhhhhhhhhhhh. Nothing at 3:00 p.m.

Day Ten: Totally depressed, hungry, and hot. My water supply was starting to take a toll as well, but should last for a week maybe. If shit got bad, I could go back to the stream, I guessed, even though I was not supposed to. Now I was getting really messed up in the head. So, many thoughts of maybe the guy taking care of me died or forgot or had a heart attack. How could I make it out of here? I had no idea where I was. I really believed that

I could die out here now. I was by myself and dying each day little by little. I wanted to give up. I admit I was broken down. *They fucking knew it!* I was at my threshold. NOTHING, NOTHING, NOTHING at 3:00 p.m.

Day Eleven: My food was almost gone. Today was the last day of anything to eat. I knew I could last weeks without any food. Did I like it? NO! The horrible head games were just killing me. I was just talking to the damn walls, wanting to throw the radio and smash it to pieces. I really was losing my damn mind. This was really getting depressing. Have they forgotten me? Why would they do this to me? I thought this was about navigation and survival. Why do they let me sit in a cabin and do nothing all day? What is this for? Nothing at 3:00 p.m.

Day Twelve: I sat around and just gave up on being heard anymore. Tired of wiping my ass with pee to clean myself. I was not officially out of food and didn't even care anymore. I just wanted someone to talk to too. Please, today be the day, please. All day I sat around waiting for 3:00 p.m. to come. It came finally, and nothing again. Now I am just fucking depressed, hot and now hungry.

Day Thirteen: I stayed in the makeshift bed and gave up on all hope. Then I started digging in the trash for wasted food that I could scrounge on. A few crumbs, rotten old cheese, and a few drops of food. Nothing to eat. I was just depressed all day. I now knew there would be no one at 3:00 p.m. I almost didn't even turn on the radio. I had zero motivation and just thought about dying in this godforsaken place alone. 3:00 p.m., nothing.

Day Fourteen: I didn't even move when the sun came up. I had no energy. I knew no one would be there at three. I knew I would never see my boys again. It was awful to be this depressed. But they got me. I looked and looked at the button, wanting to quit. I really didn't even expect anyone to even come. I would just die here. I had my camelback full, my jug full, and about two gallons left in the tank. It was truly over for me. Three p.m. came and went. I just lay down and thought of my friends and family. How I missed them all. How I deserved all of this. I was in a bad state of mind.

Day Fifteen: I just rolled over and kept thinking of my friends and family. Didn't even have the energy to poop or pee. Just drained out. Nothing to see but sand and nothing else. I was mentally done. They won, They beat me. What do I do now? Why are they doing this to me? I showed them I could survive and navigate. Why why why why why why?! Three p.m. came, and fuck me. They said go to the next point. Holy shit! They didn't die, and I was going home. OMG! I am going home, I am going home, I am going home.

I found a burst of energy and grabbed my shit and left. I looked at my arrow in the ground and headed off. After about three hours, I made it. found the flag easily. I was safe and home. I opened the can, expecting to find the note would say push the button and wait. NNNNNNNNNNNNNNNOon-nooooooooooooooooooo! It was another grid coordinate. Why why why why why! Nnoo-nnoo-nnoo-nnoo, this can't be! I was supposed to go home today.

I found little hope in my legs and mind right now. I plotted my next coordinate, hoping that was the last. It took me east for ten miles. I just picked up my stuff and headed out. I was really hoping this would be the last point. I was just worn out.

I walked slowly and moved as best I could through the sand, just depressed to all hell. I walked for about four miles, and the sun was coming up. I guess my movements were even slower than expected. I just didn't have any drive left in me. For some reason I thought this was never going to end.

I put my stakes in the ground and made an arrow pointing in the direction I was supposed to head out the next night. But this was different, no shade and nowhere to hang my poncho. I had to use my little sticks for that. So I did the best I could and dug down into the sand and made myself a foxhole about two feet deep. The stakes gave me another two feet, so I was approximately four feet under my hanging poncho.

The day came and went. Didn't get much sleep at all. I crawled out around 3:00 p.m., looked around, and packed up the bag and moved out. I still had six miles or so to the next site, and it didn't look like a whole lot of landmarks on the map. That made it even harder for me to navigate.

MONSTER

Six miles came, and nothing to see. Again, I'd missed the mark, but this time by how much? I had no visual landmarks to help me find the flag. Just sand and flat land. I put my stick in the ground and walked as far away as I could see it in one direction and started making a big circle. I made it back to the spot where I'd started, and nothing or no flag I could see in any direction. I must have really missed the point this time. I could be way off by miles.

I went back to the sock and stick and walked up about three hundred yards and placed it again. I went back north another two hundred yards so I could see the stick and did my circle again. Nothing. I was getting very discouraged. I decided to go back to the original sock-stick point and this time go south. I walked about three hundred yards and stuck the stick in the ground and did my circle. Nothing again. What the hell? I covered hundreds of yards in all directions. What do I do now? I just looked around. I thought about something I said earlier. I was right handed, so if I continued trying to walk in a straight line, I would walk in a right-handed circle because my right leg is more developed. Maybe this was it.

I went back to my original point and looked. I needed to walk northeast for about five hundred yards and look there. I walked northeast and placed my stick in the ground. By now I could see much farther because of the light. I made it out about 350 yards or so and started in my circle. I didn't make it more than a hundred yards, and I could see the flag. I was ecstatic, to say the least. This one was the toughest one yet.

I didn't even care if there was a coordinate or not. I was just happy I found it. My water supply was getting low. Hopefully they would send me to water soon. I opened the can to find some snacks and water, about a gallon of it. I was so relieved that I thanked them over and over again. Brainwashing bastards. Here I am thanking them for food and water like a child. They had me.

Of course, another coordinate. This time I was heading north again. I was so turned around because they were sending me in all directions, but I didn't care. I plotted out my course on the map, and again it was about eight miles. By the looks of it, I would see mountains and maybe more vegetation. But the great part was I could see the flag was on a mountain. This would really make it easier to find.

I dug my hole and shut it down for a while. I was exhausted and needed some shut-eye. I got some good sleep this time. Had some snacks and water and felt good today. Easy flag to find and maybe this would be it.

I started off in the northern direction doing my usual steps and keeping track of how far I moved. But things were starting to get weird. I saw way too many clouds in the distance, and this was not good. Well, some of it was. I could use my poncho to catch some water, but I could not navigate much longer. I couldn't see my stars. This posed a problem.

I decided to just hang where I was and shut down even though I had hours left and had only made about three miles or so. I couldn't chance being off my mark too much. Not now!

I dug out my hole and put the poncho on it with the hood placed in the middle; just in case the rain came, I could drip it into my jug. I had a plan. But like all plans, nothing went right. Hours and hours went by, and no water. Just clouds. I couldn't navigate, I couldn't get more water, so I just sat there. Which was bad for me because of my mind playing games with me.

I sat there thinking about what was happening to me and why. I guessed it was just my luck. Unfortunately, even in the daytime I did not want to deviate and move. I knew I would run out of water sooner and wasn't sure how long the trek to the next point of water would be. I did go out and shoot me a good azimuth with the sun and then bedded down again until 3:00 p.m.

The time was right, and I was anxious to go home. I was hoping anyway. I had made it to the mountains and was within half a mile of my flag. Even though I could see I was off, I kept on course until I hit the eight-mile mark. After that, I stuck the stick in the ground, looked around, and checked the map to see which mountain had the flag. I figured I knew which one it was, so I picked up the stick and moved about five hundred yards to the east and moved up the mountain. It was not a hard climb, I supposed. I was excited to get there and was hoping for a helicopter to land and pick me up.

I could see the flag and went over to it. Hoping of course for food and water, like a dog to his master. I opened the can quickly and found nothing but the note. Fuck! Yep, and a gosh damn coordinate. I was totally depressed. This was so old, and I just wanted to go home.

How could they keep doing this to me? I made it this far, damn it. Why would they keep doing this to me? If my master were around, this is the damn time I would turn on him and bite the shit out of his leg.

I sat down and plotted my next course and remained in disbelief. I could see I had four miles of tracking through these mountains. I was exhausted, tired, and mentally just fucked!

I started walking northwest this time. I just hung my head low and thought about all kinds of stuff. By the time I knew it, I had walked quite a bit, and fuck if I hadn't forgotten to keep accurate count. My head was not in the game anymore. Now I was really fucked. Do I go back? Start over? Or try and find my way on the map without knowing how far I came? This was the question. How could I just forget to tie knots? My mind was just not there. I was tired and exhausted, damn it.

I studied the map and mountains and had an idea where I was. But again, I wasn't totally sure. I knew what direction I was going and about how far I was. I knew the flag was in a canyon ahead of me. Somewhere, anyway. Although a lot of the mountains looked somewhat the same. I really didn't want to go back. I had to use my best judgment.

I kept going, and hell with going back. I made it to the canyon where I thought I needed to be. I looked around and again didn't see shit. This time I had a different plan. I was going to sleep until daylight so I could see better and walk up and down the canyon to be able to see the flag better. I knew I was going to consume more water, but maybe the canyon had water in there. I was down to my camelback, and that was it. I had no choice but to try this method.

When daylight came, I was on the move. I thought I would head east and look that way first for about five hundred yards. Judging from the contours on the map, this was the best chance. After a few hundred yards, I could see the flag and the fucking stupid can. But also, I could see some vegetation, which meant water.

I made it down the canyon to the can and was ecstatic to see shit pools of water. Great, another shitting fest for me. But this time I would boil the shit out of the water and not do a half-ass job like before.

I opened the can and found a note. This note said: *One coordinate will lead you to home, and the other will lead you to many more coordinates. Once you leave for the direction you are going, there will be no turning back. Use your best judgment.*

OMG, which way do I go? How do I use my best judgment on this? I'm telling you, I was terrified of picking the wrong direction to go. I knew my luck was shitty and I was going to be out for another month because I chose poorly. I had a 50 percent chance of choosing the right direction, but I felt that my actual chance was 10 percent. I was not thinking clearly at all.

I decided to stay here for a day or so and try to see what they were trying to do to me. I boiled water and boiled water until I was full that night. I found some scorpions and a small snake to eat. I cooked them crispy and ate like a king. I was so confused about what to do. I really studied the map. One led me out to the desert again about six miles or so. The other led me over the mountains to the mountaintop about six miles away. Which one, and why those two points?

I thought about this most of the night. I knew if they had to pick me up in the sand, that would be bad for the helicopter, and if they picked me up on the mountain that would be better. But is this what they were after? The mountain track was harder and closer to the sun, and I would use more water, while the desert was flat and would use less water. The mountain track was up and down and side to side because of the ravines, while the desert track was straight down and less complicated.

I really had no idea which way to go. The fact is I just didn't want to take the wrong route and have to go on. I just wanted it to all end. I stayed there the next day and tried to get my head clear to make the right judgment. What if they both were the end? Maybe they were just messing with me to keep me here wondering which way to go. They must have known my fatigue. They must!

I could not make a decision to save my life. I decided to go through the mountains because I could find food and water regardless of what happened at that point. This is the direction I was headed in.

At 3:00 p.m. I headed in the direction of the mountain, totally exhausted, mentally exhausted, and just wanting to quit. I knew if I went there and found a coordinate, I was done for. Not sure if I could go on or not.

It was about daybreak when I made it to my spot. I could see the flag up ahead and really knew it would have a coordinate in there. I knew it would. Do I quit or move on? I thought as I walked up to the flag. I was excited and scared all at the same moment.

I opened the can and saw some peanuts and water inside. I knew what this meant. As I opened the note, I saw a coordinate. I died inside. I literally was at my end. I just put it back in the can and lay there. I wanted to cry. I was sooo depressed I couldn't stand myself. I stunk like week-old piss and just wanted to die.

After a few hours of lying there mad at myself for guessing wrong, I plotted the coordinate. It looked like two miles of travel. I guess I can do that, I told myself. Not sure how many more I can go. But what is a couple of miles to the next coordinate? I looked at the map and got my bearing and started off. I could make it before daylight.

I walked and walked to try and make it to bed down for the next hike. After an hour, I guess, I made it to the flag and can, which I called the fucking can by then. I just sat there and said, "Fuck it, not opening it until tomorrow." I just couldn't bear it at this time. So I lay down for a while.

It was daylight, and I needed to get out of the sun, so I opened the can and saw some water and a protein bar. Again I was thanking them brainwashing bastards. I opened the note to see this message: *Push the button. Not allowed to speak.* OMG! Really? I love these guys! I love you, I love you, I thought. Again, brainwashing bastards.

I sat there for about three hours or so, and I could hear the copter coming. I thought to myself, I am going to have a good dinner, talk to the old fucker again, have my rundown of the events, and go to a nice hotel and then go home. Oh yes, not talk to anyone. I was done! Yay, yay!

I walked over to the copter, climbed in, and stuck out my arm like, "Let's get the show on the road, fucker." Out I went.

Chapter 6

TEST 3C FINAL: NAVIGATIONS/ SURVIVAL (ISOLATION JUNGLE)

OMG. FUUUUUUCKKKKK YYYYYOOOO-OUUUUU. I woke up to bites all over me, in the middle of the fucking jungle. *No fucking way. No fucking way.* I *hate* you mf's. I can't do this anymore! What's next, a fucking island or stuck out at sea? I HATE YOU!

I immediately had to get up and get all the damn bugs off me. They were biting the shit out of me. I looked around and realized I was in the middle of a fucking rainforest. I had no idea where the hell I was. I was next to some slough (slow-moving river), and this was where they dropped me off. I just couldn't believe this crap.

After getting all the crap off of me. I stood there just looking, and the depression was in full. I was just at the end of my rope. I really thought I was done with this. Why now the jungle? Haven't I proved my worth? It would appear not. I was in some deep-ass rainforest. I just couldn't believe it. This was not just some jungle, but looked like the Amazon. All I needed now was some headhunters to find me. I just couldn't believe it.

Wouldn't be a good day without the fucking can. The worst thing was I woke up with the same stinking-ass clothes I had on in the desert. Not a change of anything. Really, this sucks. Well, let's see what is in store for me now, and what they have for me.

I investigated the can and say the dreaded note. It stated as follows: *You will find a GPS and additional batteries in your pack. It has four points marked in them, named point 1, 2, 3, 4. After you get to the fourth point, you will be instructed what to do next.*

I was so pissed right now. I opened the pack up to see what they gave me now:

1. Glock 45 with three mags
2. Poncho with Woobie
3. One hundred feet of paracord
4. My big knife
5. Machete
6. Two changes of socks
7. Garbage sack (heavy duty)
8. Compass
9. Hat
10. Canteen cup
11. Matches

12. Flint
13. Malaria tablets for two months (two fucking months)
14. NO FUCKING BUG SPRAY!
15. GPS with sixteen extra batteries
16. The button
17. Fifteen protein bars
18. Flashlight with several batteries

I had my camelback as normal, my pack to carry everything in. I put the garbage bag in first and spread it around to keep everything dry as I could. I put in my gear and put my sidearm on my belt with clips.

I looked at the GPS, a very topographical kind, which was nice. I tried to zoom it out, but for some reason, it only let me go out two miles. Of course they did that! The first point was approximately three miles ahead. OK, I thought, I could do this. What is three miles?

I shot my compass azimuth to conserve battery life and headed out into the jungle. I knew I had to be careful because if this was the Amazon, they had some nasty creature. Piranhas, crocs, bull head sharks, all kinds of snakes (including big-ass anacondas), spiders, and ants, not to mention jaguars. But the good thing was there'd be lots of water and food I could gather.

I started off heading in the direction of the next point. The first few hundred yards were not so bad. However, it soon got bad. I couldn't see more than ten feet in front of me. I took out the machete and started hacking so I could walk and hopefully not get bitten by anything. I did not like this at all. This was a dense jungle. Remember that I was just coming out of the desert and starving, so I needed to see if there was anything I could scrounge up during the move. Again, not sure where I really was. I did assume the Amazon, though.

I hacked and hacked for a while, wearing myself completely out. I was so tired of having no food and having to cut my way through this dense jungle. I was really pissed by this point. I cut my way for about one hundred yards before it opened up a little and I was out of this thick brush. I really should have tried another direction, but too late now. Good find, though; I found a cupuaçu fruit. It's full of vitamins. At least I thought this was it. It had been a while since I studied the rainforest and edible plants and fruits. But I was sure this was it. In the military they taught us what to do if you don't know for sure: Take some juice and rub it on your inner wrist and wait for a few minutes to see if you get any irritants from it. If not, put one in your mouth and chew it and spit it out. Wait a few and then if nothing happens, eat a little bit and wait. If you don't feel sick after an hour or so, you should be good to go. I knew what I had here, so I ate one and stuffed four or so in my pack for later. Boy, did it taste good.

I kept trying to make my way through this dense jungle, and the worst part was it was daylight, but the tree cover did not help with sight. I knew in the night it would be dark, and I had to just wait till morning to move out again. No way I could move at night with all the toxic animals out there. It would be a death sentence.

MONSTER

I went on for a few more hundred yards when I came upon a snake and realized it was a coral snake. I remember the old saying "Red touches black, friend of Jack; red touches yellow, kill a fellow." Not good! This one has toxic venom, and I would die if I got bit. Not good at all. I gave him or her plenty of room and kept on walking. I didn't even try and kill it. I was good with leaving that one alive.

I kept on trucking and made my way about a mile or so. I thought now would be a good place to stop and check the GPS. I had just enough open area that I should get a satellite signal. I picked up on three satellites and had my location. I was within 1.8 miles of my destination. Not too bad, I thought.

I shot my compass heading and headed out again. Not sure what time it was; I had no watch. Bastards. I found myself in a thicker brush, which was really taking a toll on me. I kept on cutting and trying to find the end of this and get to the point so I could shut it down for the night.

After about an hour or so, I made it to somewhat of a clearing—not much, but a good place to call it a night. I was just tired and exhausted, and in this place at least I could see a little bit. The ground was totally wet and not a good place to lie, but I really had no choice in the matter.

I cut down some bamboo and tried to get myself off the ground as best I could. I then put down some big leaves, trying to make mattress so I could sleep a little bit. I noticed lots of ants roaming around and needed a fire to try and keep them away as much as possible. I already had many bites from the mosquitoes and figured malaria was on its way. Little did I know I had been taking malaria pills already for two weeks in the cabin in the desert. Yes, I found that out later; they were in my MREs, sneaky-ass bastards. But still the bugs were driving me nuts and biting me everywhere. I had to make a fire. Which is hard in the *fucking rainforest*!

I went over to a tree and dug through the bark and tried to get as much inner bark as I could that was dry. This would be my kindling. Also, it was very hard to find dry wood. But lo and behold, the rain started. So, all I could do was put up my poncho and lie on my logs for the night. I suffered this night.

The night was beautiful if you took out the bugs. I must have been a smorgasbord to them. I lost about a gallon of blood, I think. Miserable night, miserable night. But being in the rainforest, you can hear everything moving and making noise. Not a dull moment at all. If I'd had a net, I would have really enjoyed myself. But the constant biting and itching was too much for me to enjoy anything.

I put on my GPS and saw my direction, then pulled out the compass and started in my direction with my machete in the other hand. I cut and cut and actually made good progress. I came up to a waterfall and thought this was a good place to gather some water. I knew I couldn't boil any—no fire. So I dug in the ground next to the creek and let the water soak in for a little while. I then drank a bunch and filled up my pack. Not bad and tasted great.

I realized that I had to go around this paradise and get to the back side. I should have camped here for the night and should have taken a shower. What the hell—I had all day to make it three hundred yards. So I stripped down and washed up. Afterward I got out and just dried myself off by dripping. It really felt refreshing. No big anacondas here. Thank you.

I finally got dressed and hoofed it around the little mountain and regained my direction and made it to the point. Nice, I thought. Not too bad, but bad enough. I opened the can in the clearing where it was placed and wondered how they got it here. I assumed with a copter and rope. That was the only way I could see that happening.

I opened the can and looked inside, not really knowing what to expect because I already had the coordinates in the GPS. I found a laminated card with pictures of some plants and fruits that were edible. Well, that was nice of them, I thought, because I couldn't remember everything. Not sure how to take that. Maybe they are helping me make it after all. Maybe?

I looked at the GPS and saw I had about a four-mile hike and a big-ass river in front of me. I couldn't really see the whole river, though, because they'd blocked my GPS from zooming out. This I didn't like at all. As I zoomed out on the GPS, I could see no way to cross this thing but swim. I really did not like this and was really worried, mostly because of everything that was in that river that could kill me.

I made it to the river and looked at it in disbelief. Wow, very big, I thought, and no way around but through it. I had to make a raft of some kind, and that could help me. I used some of my paracord and made a raft out of some smaller trees as best I could. I took off my shoes, pants, and shirt and put them in my pack to try and keep as dry as possible. I found a big bamboo that I cut into a paddle and sat my ass down, and of course I sank in about a foot or so. But good enough I thought.

I slowly made my way across this gentle, giant river. I could see fish or something making some waves of sorts. I kept thinking of big-ass snakes or gators. I wasn't sure what they were. I did not like having my feet in there, but I really had no choice. I just gave it my all and kept positive and moved on.

I finally made it to the other side and with relatively no issues. I untied my paracord to use later. I got my butt dressed and was ready to move on. I still had about 3.4 miles to go. So, I did my usual and got my heading and started out. Not so bad at first until I saw a footprint of a cat. A big footprint. I knew what that was and didn't like that at all. I'd heard stories of natives who wore masks on the back of their heads because the cats would not attack you from the front. So, if they saw a mask on backward, they were confused and left you alone. I was not sure how true that was but really wished I had a mask.

I made my way through the jungle and prayed I didn't see one. I had my sidearm but was still not too interested in this deal. They hang out in the trees and could just jump my stupid ass for being out here. Which wouldn't be too bad; at least I could die and get this over. LOL.

I checked my compass, but while I was sitting there, I saw bananas. You have got to be kidding me. I jumped up and started over to them. This was awesome. Then I heard a horrible noise and looked up, expecting to be eaten by the cat. But no, it was monkeys, howler monkeys, and they seemed pissed I was there. I stopped and chatted with them for a minute. I wanted them to know that I was not there to hurt them and just kept quiet for a minute and watched them. I'd heard stories of them in wartime. They would make howling noise when troops were walking by, and that's how the other troops knew where they were. Interesting fact. I was not so sure it was true but did like the story.

I grabbed a bunch of bananas and truly was excited to eat them. It was a little hard to find ones that were ready to eat. I found some close enough for that. I sat down and looked at the monkeys and ate two of them and had about fifteen more to ripen in my bag. I just sat there and talked to the monkeys as they screamed at me. After I'd spent about an hour resting, they seemed to be staring at me just as much as I was at them. They didn't make as much noise. Maybe they understood I wasn't there to hurt them. To be honest, I enjoyed their company. I guess it had been so long since I had a conversation that even a monkey sufficed.

It was time to move on. I actually thought about staying here for the night and having some company. God, I am a loser. It was really nice to sit and watch them hanging around and looking at me. I enjoyed them, and if I had more time, I would have given them names. I had to keep going, though, and hope I would run into more later.

As I made my way to the next point, I could see it looked as though I was going in a big circle, which didn't make sense to me at all. If I could have zoomed out on the GPS, I would have been able to see what was going on. But whatever, I thought.

Finally, about a mile from the point, I had a thought. I turned on the GPS, and fuck me. *The same fucking river was in front of me.* Them bastards are making me cross the same damn river again to get back to the other side. I am so pissed right now. I must be a mile or so from my last crossing. But who knows? I can't see in the GPS far enough to tell. I am pissed!

Well, I came to the river, and the point was just on the other side of it. Maybe a hundred yards or so but I had to cross the river again. This time I was going to take my time and make a raft that would support my legs to keep them out of the water. No more messing around; I had to be safe.

I took my time and made a big ole raft and used a lot of paracord, but that was OK. I really didn't want to have my feet in the water this time. I looked around to make sure there were no crocs or big snakes. I didn't see any slides from bellies from the crocs, so I thought I was OK. Plus, the water was moving a little bit faster. I know they like slow-moving water best. Although this wasn't rapids, it just seemed faster.

I slowly put in my raft and have to say it was a pretty sturdy one. I did a good job on this one. I made a decent paddle and was ready. I took off my clothes and put them in the bag and headed into the water. I was trucking right along and not taking my time, I can say that. However, I was not in too big of a hurry to cause noise or stir up the water. Just enough to get me across. Again, I saw things making some water move in there. Not happy with that at all. I was not sure if that was a snake, a croc, or some big-ass fish.

I made it to the other side and was very grateful that nothing ate me. I undid my raft and packed everything away and finished dressing. I made my way to the next point rather easily. It was sitting in a nice open spot. Of course, when I say open, that means I could see the sky a little bit. Just enough to get a GPS satellite coordinate.

I opened the box to find a small bottle of bug lotion. Man, these guys love me, I thought. Then of course the thought came in again: brainwashing bastards! I read the note saying go to next coordinate.

I turned on the GPS, and it looked like I had to go about five miles or so. Unfortunately, I could only see one damn mile ahead of me. Now, I didn't know what to expect. If I had to cross that river again, I was going to lose my mind. The good note was I was down for the night.

It was a good place to chill out and rest. I cut some vines and drank the water from them. I had done this many times before. So I knew this was OK. Also, you can tie pieces of clothing around your boots and walk around to suck up the morning dew and then ring them out in your cup. Also, a good way to gather water in the jungle. The best way is to wait for the rain to come again. Tie your poncho up with the head part in the middle and leave it untied. Let the water drip in your cup and keep filling your camelback. This is fast and easy in the jungle because it rains a lot.

Water and food were not a big deal in the jungle. The problem really lay with setting fires and keeping myself dry—which I was not doing so well at. Also foot rot (immersion foot) is common in the jungle. I did not want that. I tried to keep my feet as dry as possible and changed my socks and let the others air-dry often.

The biggest problem that I was having, which was weird to me, was isolation and claustrophobia. When you can only see ten to twenty feet all day long, it gets old and somewhat scary. You never know what is in front or behind you. You just can't see anything far away. I was not really used to this at all.

The sounds in the jungle can be beautiful and peaceful; however, they can also be terrifying. Throughout this small ordeal I heard all kinds of weird noises that were quite upsetting to me. I had no clue what they were. Also, I felt like I was being watched every minute of the day. I did not like this feeling at all.

I made a makeshift bed. I placed some big logs on the ground about four feet long and about ten inches in diameter. Next, I put logs lengthwise, and this kept me off the ground enough to stay away from the ants and crawly things. I gathered up some big leaves to try and make a mattress. It was better than bare logs anyway. I was hoping anyway. My gracious keepers had given me bug lotion. This was awesome; I could put some on sparingly and use my poncho over the top of me and hopefully have a decent night.

The night was fucking miserable. I had just as many bites as the night before. I have no idea how they got in and ate the shit out of me, but I did not sleep very much. Good thing nothing on the penis; I guess they couldn't find it. LOL.

I got up and cleared myself off and recovered my items. I was so miserable and scratching that it was literally driving me nuts. The insects were still out and about, biting the shit out of me. In my ears, mouth, and butt crack. It was almost unbearable.

I was out headed to my next point, and this was not a good point at all. I was hacking and hacking my way through deep brush and couldn't see two feet in front of me. I was so tired and exhausted. I was not making good progress at all. It was like they picked the worst point in the middle of the densest part of the jungle to go to.

After three hours I was still not making much progress and was really miserable. I couldn't see anything and was extremely tired. I couldn't even find a good place to sit. It was really dense, and I was just tired. I probably made about a half mile at tops. It was really bad, and I couldn't see any end in sight. The tree canopy over the top was completely covered. No sun and of course the rain had started in.

I put my poncho over me, trying to stay dry, but my pants and shoes were really soaked. This was the worst track yet. Completely wet, tired, exhausted, and miserable.

After resting and eating to gain some strength back, I started in again. I hacked for another few hours without seeing an end to this mess. I was on the verge of just giving up. I was mentally exhausted and tired of trying to prove my worth to these people. They were very close to winning the game with me. I just wanted to quit and go home and just go to work and live a normal life.

After about another hour and making slower and slower progress, I was out of the brush and could at least see a few more feet in front of me. I found somewhat of an opening in the trees and tried to get a GPS reading. It looked as though I had only gone about three hundred yards the whole day. How could this be?

I had not even made a mile in one full day and needed to shut it down for the night. I didn't even care at that point. I was just exhausted and again mentally drained. I made my bed, a shitty one this time. I just didn't have it in me to work any harder. I ate a protein bar and bananas and drank water. Put the lotion on and crashed out. I actually slept pretty hard this night. Of course, I woke up to more bites and itched myself to death. The problem that I saw coming was my wet feet and scratching so much to cause the bites to bleed. My body was a mess at this time.

I slowly packed up my stuff, whipped off the bugs, and just hung my head down low and started walking. I didn't have to cut my brush down, just some low-hanging branches and stuff. I was making better time, but I was really down and disappointed in everything. I guess it was because the last two missions in the mountains and desert just took a toll on me, and I didn't see the end in sight.

I had really no motivation at all, just hanging on by a thread. Wished I could just get out of this jungle; the solitude was driving me really nuts by this point. I wished

I could find more monkeys. I know that sounds stupid, but I was very lonely and depressed. I just wanted to talk to something and see if I could find the motivation to keep going.

I spent most of the day avoiding snakes and eating whatever I could find and drinking plenty of water. I was making some time up from the bush but not enough to make it to the next point. I still had about two miles to go, and one more point after that. I just couldn't see an end to this madness. I was losing my ever-loving mind.

I found a good place to call it quits again. I tried to make a better bed this time and tried to make a fire. After a few attempts, I just quit. Everything was so wet, and I really didn't want to go the extra mile at this point. I could have made one if I tried harder, but I just couldn't find it in me.

I tried to sleep as best as I could. Not easy with insects all over your body and buzzing in your ears. I was really trying not to use my repellent much; I only had a small amount of it.

I had taken off my boots to try and dry my feet as best as I could. But I could tell they were getting in bad shape and if I didn't get them dry, immersion foot was coming. They were already starting to hurt. I just couldn't keep them dry, and without a fire there was no hope. I wasn't even sure I could make another mile or even two. I was in a rough shape. I needed to stop tomorrow and build a fire and dry it out. What I really needed was a cave of some sort.

I was going to try and make it to the next point, but if I couldn't make good time, then I was going to find a place and take my time and build a fire. I needed to dry out really bad, or I was done. I knew this routine and needed to do just that. I knew how to survive in the jungle but needed to slow down and heal up. So that was the plan moving forward.

I started out and moved along slowly, and my feet hurt. I just needed a good place to make it to. After about 1.5 miles, I found just the place. I was done and could spend quality time making a fire. I found some good overhang so I could stay out of the rain and hopefully make a good fire.

I took my time and gathered lots of kindling. I scraped the inside of the barks till I had a pile of it. I cut the bark into small pieces to throw onto the fire after it was lit and then gathered some more branches. I did everything by the numbers on this one. I could not fail; if I did, I was out. I looked for the deadest wood I could find and gathered it up. Next, I found big leaves of some sort and tied two branches about five feet or so above the fire and then put lots of leaves over the branches to keep the rain out. I really took my time to make everything perfect before I attempted to start it.

After getting everything set up, I needed to make a bed to sit off the ground so I could dry myself out. I have to say the bed was perfect this time, under the canopy, off the ground, and not many ants snooping around this area. I was ready.

I took out one match and lit the tinder on fire. It went perfectly, and I kept adding branches. All was great, and the warmth felt awesome. I put out forked branches in the ground to hang up the socks and boots. Those had to get dry first. Everything was going as planned. My socks and feet were drying out nicely. I was going to make it. Surprisingly enough, no rain that night and not a lot of bugs. I guess because of the fire. Fire is the one thing that is important to survival. It gives you security from animals, comfort, and a will to move on.

That night was really what I needed, and I felt refreshed and alive again. I had gained some motivation back and some mental health too. I needed that fire more than anything. What a feeling to have a fire at the right time. I was ready to find the next point. All dry and ready to go.

I finally made it to the next point. Nice openness was great too. I opened the can and found a little thing of lighter fluid. *Are you fucking kidding me?!* But I was not complaining at all. I was happy for it and thanked them again. This would make life a lot easier for fires next time. I read the note and of course will go to the next point.

As I looked at the GPS, I could see it was only about a mile away. The terrain looked rough, but what's a mile, I thought. I started off still feeling good and made my way down this ravine. The jungle was getting really dense, and there was very little light. Even though it was light out, it was very dense and hid lots of it. I couldn't see more than five feet in front of me. I hacked a little to get through some of it. Then it appeared!

I don't even know what I thought at that moment. I was so amazed and confused and even wanted to cry from madness. How the hell did they get that here? They must have brought it in with a copter and had someone come down and put it in. I have no idea. I just wanted to cry. It was the fucking cabin.

I couldn't even imagine this was happening to me again. I was just stood there in awe. They were truly breaking me at this point. I felt like just quitting, I wasn't sure I could do another stretch in the cabin and this claustrophobic area. I just couldn't see far at all. It was a horrible feeling.

Well, it was time to see what was going on now. I opened the half-ass door that hardly even shut. The cabin was a complete dump and mess. I would say it was probably seven feet long by four feet wide and eight feet tall, not much room. It was smaller than the rest of them. I was really feeling isolated and claustrophobic in the area. I saw some MREs out of the packages on the ground that someone had stomped into the dirt. Not one of them wasn't crushed. I wonder why they did this.

The walls on the cabin had been scratched into with knives, as if someone had been counting days or something. The marks were everywhere. I was certain now that I had not been the first or last to come into this cabin hellhole. I saw the radio sitting on a stool, and after closer inspection, I noticed six white wires in the back had been cut. This made no sense at all to me. Why were they all cut and all white? Then I saw the dreaded note. It stated as follows: *After 100 days if we don't hear from you, proceed to the next coordinate.*

I looked at the coordinate and saw that they forgot to put the last number on the grids. OMG, you stupid assholes! How can I find the coordinate when you forgot the last numbers? I then thought of the radio and the wires being cut. My God, I have to try and figure out which one goes to which one. There must be a billion combinations. I was not lucky, so I knew I would be here for the entire one hundred days and that I would be insane after that. Also, after one hundred days, I still wouldn't have the coordinate. I can't believe this!

After looking around the cabin more, I could see that the walls were not all on the ground. There were two-inch gaps everywhere, and the windows had no windows. This meant the insects would eat me alive in there. I checked out the outside part and found a solar panel for the radio that didn't work perched on top. Then I walked around as much as I could and saw a cesspool of water that was an insect haven. This was not good at all. I had to get all the holes plugged up as best as I could now.

I picked up all the food. Not much of it, maybe three full MREs at best. I then took my boot and scraped the dirt and mud and packed the bottom of the walls to try and keep things out. Unfortunately, it wasn't sealed tight, but it would do for now. I then went out and cut some nice leaves to hang over the windows to keep some bugs out. I really had to find a better way; they were going to eat me alive with the cesspool of crap next to the cabin.

That was why they put it there, I was sure: just to make me as miserable as possible.

Day One: Calgon, please take me away! I spent most of the day looking at the wires and trying to figure this out. However, I had no way to mark them, so I tied strings around each one: one string for the first string, two for the second, and so forth. That way I could try and make some sense of what I was trying to do. After I hooked up all six in some random sequence, I would call out and wait. The radio made a noise and sounded like it was working, but I never heard anything back. So, I kept on and kept on. Starting to drive me nuts now. If I couldn't figure this out, I would be stuck here for one hundred days or so. Then I realized that I didn't even really know where to go. I was missing one number in the coordinate, so I could never find the next point in this dense jungle. I was really frustrated.

Well, it was time to shut it down for the night and see what the night brought to me. I hadn't been shut down for an hour or so when the bugs were coming in like I hadn't even done anything. I was constantly scratching and waving them off. Losing it, I thought to myself.

Day Two: Dear Dr. Phil, I am losing my mind out here and need some guidance. I don't know how much longer I can do this. The bugs last night were eating me alive. The cesspool is a growing bacteria mess. Please help! Figures that he never showed up or called.

MONSTER

Today I tried to make the cabin more insect free. I put up a lot of leaves on the windows and stuffed mud in all the open cracks. I looked for any light coming in, and it was pretty dark. That posed another problem: How could I see the wires like this? I took down some of the leaves so I could see during the day and then put them back at night. I figured this was the best option. Then I went outside and did the same with the bottom of the cabin. It seemed secure now.

I was still hungry and hadn't eaten any of my MREs I was saving them for a special occasion.

It was now time to forage. As I took short little walks around the cabin, I came upon some fruit-like things. I didn't recognize what they were. I went back to the cabin and grabbed that chart they gave me, and sure enough, the fruit was in there. So I picked some and ate them. This was nice. I was full but now needed water and really didn't want to drink out of the cesspool.

It appeared I hadn't a choice, so it was time to build a fire. After some time, I got one built up and boiled the piss out of the water. It tasted like piss. But what do you do? I then got a brilliant idea to filter the water with charcoal. I filled up one of my socks with charcoal from the fire and let the water filter through that as well. It was the best I could do. This did give the water some taste. Better than nothing. I filled the camelback up and went back to the cabin and started working on the radio again. I was fucking going nuts!

That night the bugs were not as bad but still there. I didn't sleep much. My mind was in bad shape. I just was losing it, staying in this little cabin all day and night. I found myself talking to the mosquitoes buzzing in my ear. I would tell them, "Oh, Morticia, I love it when you speak French to me." I was losing my mind.

Day Three: Dr. Ruth, I need your help. For some strange reason I needed a sex therapist today. For an unknown reason I became horny as hell. Don't ask me why. But after thinking of Margaret Houlihan, all was better. *Aaaaaaaaaaaaaaahhhhhhhhhhhh*. Well, now that was done, I needed to get back to the radio. I spent most of the day one wire to this wire, cussing aloud like a lunatic.

I went back outside and looked for some more damn fruit. I found another kind as well about twenty feet from the cabin. This is weird, I thought. Did they know this was here? Did they put me here because there was food for my one hundred days? Not really sure, but that is what it looks like. Then reality set in. They planned on me being here that long; they knew I couldn't fix the radio. Fuckers!

That night I lay on the ground, and fuck me, all I could think about was Ginger and Mary Ann from *Gilligan's Island*. This really sucked but you know. I had to do what I had to do. I guess it passed the time for a minute or two.

Day Four: "Tupac!" I screamed in the morning. "I want to kill something like you did! I want to kill all these damn bugs. I am losing my mind, damn it." I started talking to myself and just losing it, I guess. I was so frustrated with the radio and knowing that I didn't have the full coordinates to leave.

I had to go outside for a while and find something to do. I was not the kind of guy that could just sit around and do nothing. I had to find something, but what? I roamed around for a while and tried to find a pet to talk to. Nothing, not even a snake to kill and eat. I would have loved some protein now.

I went back to the cabin and just sat there looking at the radio wires. I seemed to have no motivation anymore. I just felt so low at this time. Just didn't know what to do. I spent most of the day connecting and reconnecting wires and screaming into the mike. Nothing, as usual.

It was time to have some crackers from the MREs. I was so thankful they had stepped on them and crushed them into crumbs. If only I had some Grey Poupon. But of course not. Just crunched-up dry crackers. I sat and stared at the radio.

Day Five: Not doing so well. Had no luck with the radio and was cussing Radar O'Reilly from *M*A*S*H* for not giving me any advice. Last night was again an insect fest on me. I was exhausted from no sleep and scratching. I went out and boiled water and saw a little guppy in the pool. I thought it was OK; I would name him Gill and put him in my canteen cup and tie it around my neck.

After some water and something to eat, I went back into the cabin and started again with the radio. All day, and nothing. Were they even fucking listening? I was screaming at the top of my lungs. I was so pissed by the end of the day. There was no way to ever get the sequence right. There were just too many wires. Why were they doing this to me? Lurch, play me a tune on the harpsichord. Nothing. Just the sound of jungle.

Day Six: Groundhog Day. I thought about a stripper named Muffy; she was superhot and a home-wrecking bitch. Now that would have been a good day to live over and over, being with her. But now all I have is Gill! *Gillllll*, I'm going to eat you! Although I wanted to, he was my only friend, so I couldn't. I would just go out and see his little ass swimming around once in a while. He was the same as me. He was stuck in a little pond of shit while I was stuck in a cabin. Maybe he was working with the government too. Spying little bastard. Probably reporting in everything I was saying. I could see his little radio calling me in. I was starting to hate that fish.

I made my way back to the cabin and had little to no motivation. I lay down and didn't even touch the radio today. I was mentally fucked. Just couldn't do anything that day. I knew I had ninety-four more days and wondered how I could even stand that. Why were they messing with me so hard? I didn't get it.

Day Seven: I couldn't get up. I lay there and thought about sex mostly. I think I would have had sex with Princess Fiona after sundown now. Not sure why sex was on my mind. Maybe because of boredom, or just loneliness. Whatever the reason was, I had no idea. So I just thought about it and lay there for another few hours.

I finally got up and went poop and peed. My only excitement for the day, although all the bug bites on my privates made me think of the stripper Muffy. It was bigger now and had lots of bumps; she could have enjoyed it now. LOL.

I did my normal routine with water and food. Went back to the cabin and screamed at the radio. Like that was going to help. Well, it did, I guess. I tried and tried more combinations with no luck. I lay back down and thought about having sex with a Klingon. My mind was losing it. Ninety-three days left. I just wanted to go to sleep.

I fell asleep and swatted flies and mosquitoes all night, screaming strange shit in the air. I just wanted to fly over the cuckoo nest.

Day Eight: I lay there in sadness, wondering why they were doing this to me. Haven't I proved myself to you people? I thought. This was definitely the hardest thing I ever went through. Even in the military there was always some asshole around. Here there was no one; I was a lost soul. Why were they doing this to me? I was mentally broken down. I had been gone for so long, and there was no one to talk to. Doing things I didn't even understand. "Ninety-two days left. Ninety-two days left. Ninety-two days left," I kept repeating.

I really didn't think this would ever end. I must be a science project for them to see how long a person can live like this, I thought. I now know that this will never end, and next time I will be in another environment and another cabin and something else will happen. This is just not normal for this type of training. I really wonder if anyone has made it, or do they just keep going until you finally quit? Is there really an end to this or not? I had to keep trying, but I was really at my end. I could not figure out the radio. I was losing my mind more and more.

I tried to fix the radio throughout the day and tried to call several times but to no avail. Nothing. I dragged my lazy ass outside and did my thing and looked down to see all the bite marks all over my body. This was not good. If they made me swim in the river, I would be eaten alive by piranhas.

Day Nine: I screamed most of the night and talked to myself for the rest. I was out of it, and I had ninety days left. I was barely in this a week and was not doing good. How was I going to make it? If I thought this was it, I might be able to. But unknowing if this was it or not drove me crazier. I really wanted to pass this test, but how much longer would it go on? If only I had an end in sight.

I spent the day talking and rambling on about various stuff and studying the radio, trying and trying to get it to work. Just nothing I tried seeming to work. I went outside for a while and talked to Gill. I assumed he thought I was nuts too. I found some good fruit and sat and ate. To be honest, I just wanted it to fucking end.

Day Ten: I was lying there looking at the radio when I heard the most god-awful scream. What the hell was that?! Not sure if this was a monkey or a leopard. This did make me somewhat excited that something was around and somewhat a little uneasy. But it was something new. I grabbed the 45 and went out. Unfortunately, I couldn't see very far. At this point I didn't even care. I just wanted to shoot something or be eaten. Where oh where are you? I screamed out like a mad man, "Come out!" Nothing, it must be related to the radio. Whatever it had screamed, it was not there anymore. I decided to go and look for it.

I grabbed the GPS just in case I got lost and headed out. I didn't go too far from home but farther than I had before. Fuck me! I found a little creek, and the water was way better than Gill's Pond. I was around a hundred feet or so from the cabin. I took the machete and made marks going back so I could find this spot again. I grabbed my canteen cup and filled it. Then I went back to my makeshift fire spot, which was covered so the rain couldn't get to it, and built another fire.

I trekked back and forth and filled up my camelback, and then I saw something move in the water. It looked like a fish of some sort. Game on, fishy poo! I went to the nearest tree and cut down a stick to use to stab this fish. I was hungry, and he was going to die. I needed meat. This also gave me hope and energy. I needed this. It was something to do beside the radio that didn't work.

I stabbed and stabbed until I finally felt the poke. I got him, I thought. I was not really sure what he was, but it was a fish of some sort, and I was eating him tonight. I went back and cooked him up. I felt great and now game on for that stream. It gave me hope.

After eating the fish and drinking better water, I started on the radio again. Just like every other day, nothing. I was back to being discouraged again and feeling depressed. Damn it.

Day Eleven: The bugs kept coming and coming. Today was going to be different. I decided to build a small fire in the cabin and let the smoke out the window to see if that was a deterrence for them tonight. I spent most of the morning trying to get another fish, but again nothing. I didn't even see anything even though I ventured up the creek a way. Oh well, back to the radio.

I spent most of the day cussing and acting like an idiot. Then it hit again, the horniness. Why am I getting this way out here? I thought. Well, you know what happened after a few minutes. That's right, back at the radio. Nothing. I went back out and grabbed some fruit and looked for another fish. No fish but fruit, yes.

I started a little fire in the cabin with some of my dry wood, and smoke went up and out the window. This was brilliant! But before too long, I could see the smoke coming down and filling up the cabin. I had to stomp out the fire and open the door. Maybe that wasn't such a good idea. Maybe I needed a hole in the top. But it would also be stupid to let the rain in. I was struggling.

Day Twelve: Depressed and lonely and wet. It was a bad storm last night, and the rain kept coming in and soaking me. Now I was more miserable and had to try and fix the cabin better. Just too much rain last night.

I opened the door and found that the pond where Gill stayed was now full and at the door. This wasn't good.

It must have really rained last night. Of course, my feet were wet again and most of the clothing and all my fire stuff completely soaked. This is bad, I thought. My floor in the cabin was mud pie. So now what? I needed to dry myself off somehow. But for the life of me, I just couldn't find the answer. I took off my socks and shoes and sat there most of the day playing with the radio, screaming obscenities.

It was getting nighttime, and everything was still wet. It was going to be a miserable night. But what else was new? I kept telling Morticia to leave me the hell alone. I didn't care about French anymore. But no, she kept it up all night. I wanted to punch Pugsley in the mouth as well. Why am I thinking of the Addams family right now? I wondered. Hell, I'd probably have sex with Gomez right now. LOL. I still didn't understand the drive for sex when you're so miserable. I guess there is just nothing else to think about.

Day Thirteen: My life sucks. This is never going to end. Here it is day thirteen, and I have eighty-seven more to go. Being out in the field is nothing, but usually you are with someone else. But being by yourself in a jungle is totally different. I lost all morale, motivation, mental health, and my body ached. I had to get dry today.

I went out into the jungle and went to the stream and bathed. It really was refreshing, and I didn't see anything to eat in it. But that was OK; I had fruit of sorts to choose from. I peeled bark off to make a fire and finally got one started. I sat there cleaning my water and drying my clothes. It gave me some sort of hope. This was by far the worst obstacle yet. Just not knowing anything and not much chance of finding the next point. I only wished they knew I didn't have the last full coordinate. Who knows; maybe they did and would drop it out of a helicopter.

I spent the rest of the day on the radio. I was running out of ideas. Why did they have all the same colors. Just to mess with me? Did they even know the radio was broken and the coordinate didn't have the last numbers? I lay down in the mud and went to sleep.

Day Fourteen: "I want to die." I kept saying it over and over. "Just let me die and get it over with." But I had one thing that kept me going. My boys. I couldn't go out without saying goodbye. Besides, they were not going to win. I am not the kind to lie down and quit. Today is the day I eat, drink, and fix the radio!

I went back out to the creek and found a small fish. I got him quickly. I must have been getting better at killing. He tasted so good. My luck was changing, and now it was time to fix the radio. No matter what happened, that damn radio was going to get fixed—if not today, then tomorrow.

Day Fifteen: I am alive and today is the day to fix the radio, I told myself. The boys' daddy is coming home. I went out and started a fire and filled my water and ate some of the MREs. I felt alive today. I kept telling them assholes they were not going to win and if I had to stay here one hundred days, then so be it. I was getting used to this shit and loving the adventure.

I tried the radio, and I heard something on the other end. Sounded like six and three. Could that be the last coordinate number? I repeated, "Did you say six and three?" It came back, "Yes, six and three." I think I shit my pants. My shriveled-up penis came alive and told me to get my shit and move.

I put the coordinates in and saw I had about 1.5 miles to walk, and I started off. I was so happy that I couldn't stand it. I made good time walking to the next point. However, the day was coming to an end, and I had to get there and bed down for the night. But who cared? I was out of the cabin.

I made it to the point, and there was a nice flag and can and a big clearing. Does this mean a helicopter could land here? Oh please, let it be. I walked straight over to the can and opened it. One MRE and two bottles of water and a note. *Push the button and wait till morning.* OMG, I am leaving this shithole. I was ecstatic.

That night I couldn't even sleep; I was so happy to go on to the next adventure. I didn't care, just wanted out of here. That morning the copter came, and I stuck out my arm. He stuck me like usual and off to sleep I went. Knowing that I was going to wake up on an island or something next, I didn't care.

Chapter 7

INTERROGATION AND EXPLANATIONS: NEXT PHASE

I woke up, and to my surprise I was in a nice hotel room. Wondering how the hell I got here. But who cares. I was clean and dressed in a nice robe and lying in a soft, wonderful bed. The hell was over, I thought. I got up and noticed lots of different kinds of food on the table. Of course, it was set for two. I got up and looked outside and saw I was back in the States. How relieved I was.

Wasn't but ten minutes or so and he walked in. Yes, the same guy as before with his notepad. Here we go again, I thought. He sat across the table from me and opened up the metal pan and revealed a big ole steak. I had one too. He told me to dig in.

We sat there and ate crab legs and just bullshitted about everything but the last test. I guessed that was coming soon enough. Anyway, I enjoyed the conversation;

he actually talked somewhat of his family and was way more open than before. That also surprised me. He had never talked to me like this before nor fed me like this before. Not sure what to think.

After we were done for a little bit, he asked me to sit on the couch for our usual discussion. I was just so relieved to be treated like a person now. I was happy to chat with him.

He started in on the three tests and asked me what I thought about them. I was blunt and told him it was extremely difficult and tiresome. He agreed with me. Told me most of the candidates never made it all the way. They usually fell out from not finding points or just plain gave up. That made me feel good about myself.

He then asked me what I thought it was all about. I told him about navigation in different environments and survival. He told me that was a small part of it but not all of it. I asked him what else could it be? He said solitude and loss of hope. I thought about this for a minute and told him I sure had those feelings many times. He said, "Yes, I know."

"Yes, you know? How could you possibly know?" I asked.

He told me, "The cabins were bugged, and so was your button. We heard everything you said and did. I replied to everything. Yes, everything."

I looked at him and said, "Oh shit, sorry about the cussing and everything."

He made a little laugh and said, "You were right with the others, including myself."

"Yourself?"

"Yes," he replied. "I went through the same stuff years ago. Wasn't quite as advanced as your ordeal, but most of us do go through that training."

Oh, I felt a little weird, knowing all the stuff I'd done and said. Ouchhh!

He told me, "We actually didn't think you were going to make it a few times with your depression and exhaustion, but you pulled through. We also were very pleased with your skills and navigation. You proved to us that you are what we want in our organization."

I felt like I was on cloud nine.

He asked me what the toughest part for me was. I told him the jungle because I thought I was done after the desert. He said, "That's usually when people quit. They think after something that is hard it's over. This is why we add something else—to just give them a little more push to quit. Most do during the third phase."

He then said, "You actually thought it was over after the desert too, didn't you?"

I responded, "Well, of course I did. That test was very hard on me, and I thought I was losing my mind at one point."

"Which part?" he asked.

I said, "Once when I couldn't find the point and thought I would die of dehydration. And the cabin, of course."

"That cabin really gets to people," he said. "And yes, the thought of not knowing the end is also very hard on even the most hardened vets." Then he went on about the radio in the cabin. "I know you had some difficulties with that."

I told him, "Yes, that was extreme bullshit. I could have spent years out there and never found the combinations."

He laughed and said, "It worked the whole time. We just wanted to see if you would mentally break or not. Once you got out of your slump, we knew you were good to go."

"That pisses me off that the radio worked the whole time!" I said.

He just laughed and told me they all got a good one listening to me screaming and doing other things.

Ha-ha. I was a little embarrassed at that comment. I knew what he was talking about.

I then asked him about all the scratches in the wood. He said, "Some of the people put them there, and we did the rest to give you no hope. We wanted to break you down if we could. We need people that will not break. It's more of a head game to let you think you will be there for one hundred days."

He told me, "Don't get angry. We are very selective in our training and selecting the right people for certain areas we want them for. You did very well in all areas, and soon you will be in training. But we still need a debriefing to make things better for the next person that comes along."

"I understood that," I said.

He asked, "How'd you like the little gifts we gave you?"

I told him I liked them very much and thanked him for all of them. He graciously gave me a nod. He then proceeded to ask if there were any gifts that would have been better or worse.

"I needed water, so you sent me to that," I said. "When I was desperate for food, you led me to that. As long as my skills were up and trained, it was good enough." I thought a moment. "I guess at the time I didn't know why you gave me some things. For example, you gave me a card with pictures of edible fruits. But then again, you knew in the cabin they were there, didn't you?"

He just nodded and said, "Of course."

He went back to talking about the days in the cabin. The first time was short, the next time was longer, and the third time was longer. "What do you think about that?" he asked.

I told him the first time was fine. I had plenty of things to see, and it wasn't bad. "I was pissed that I rationed my food and then you told me to leave it all," I said.

He said we all do that.

I then said, "The next time I didn't see myself staying in there that long, so I ate good and didn't ration enough."

He laughed and said, "So did I."

"But I ran out and was really pissed."

He said, "Yes, we heard you. We knew you would be OK if you had enough water, so we made you suffer more. We wanted you as drained as we could get you before the jungle."

What an asshole, I thought. But I understood that.

He then went on about the points in the desert. He asked what I thought of the course.

I told him, "That was the hardest because I didn't have anything but the stars. And I could miss the mark by miles if I wasn't careful."

He did agree that the hardest part of the desert was finding the next mark. "This is why you were given a topographical map," he said.

"Yes, that did help a lot," I replied. "Talking about that, why did we have to make decisions, like the one where you told me to use my instincts?"

"Most would choose the easier path. But we all know that is not always the best choice."

Then I said, "You mentioned two paths: one led you to home and the other led you to other points."

He laughed again. He said they both led you to one more point. "Just wanted to see if you would give up after choosing the wrong path," he told me. "However, you kept going." He then said, "We try our best to make people quit. We don't want them; we want those that are willing to die before they quit. Those are the types of personalities we are looking for."

He asked me out of laughter about the river and the GPS next. I told him, "I actually thought about killing you when I realized I was crossing the same river."

"That is why we put a distance on the GPS," he said. "So you couldn't see that far. It always gets people fired up. But we also try and do it in a safer section of the river so you don't get eaten. See how we look out for you?"

I agreed and thanked him again for that.

He then came out and said that people who talk to themselves usually have higher intelligence. He said, "You must be a genius as much as you talked to yourself." He laughed. "It helps us see how you are doing when you do that and how bad you are doing. With you we knew all the time what you were thinking and doing."

Again, I felt embarrassed. He looked at me and said, "Don't feel embarrassed. We all do it."

"Do *it*? I asked.

He said, "Yes. DO IT."

I knew what he was talking about then.

He said, "Maybe I should go find Muffy and take out some frustrations."

Oh…

He was wrapping it up and said that I am into the system now and the next step is the training. No more test; I was done with that. He told me I should be proud of my accomplishments. A nice bonus would be intact, and I should go on vacation for a while and recover before going back to work. I agreed that would be nice. He told me I looked like hell and needed at least three weeks to gain weight back and get rid of all the bites. He told me they would give me a few more shots to help me recover faster.

I agreed. "Do whatever you all think is best."

He said, "Good answer." He then told me the next few times we met would be for intense training.

Of course, I asked what kind.

He just said, "The kind that will help you stay alive."

MONSTER

So, I left it at that and sat there. It was evident he wasn't going to spoil the surprise. But before he left, he again told me what a great service I was going to do for my country. It made me feel great inside knowing that I was helping my country again and doing what needed to be done. Little did I know what I was about to become. The most hideous creature on the planet. A true unrecognizable monster.

Chapter 8

TRAINING TO BECOME THE MONSTER

Life was all good. For the next few months, I was doing well, spending time with my boys and working. I know I was excited to be part of the future of protecting the country and doing what was asked of me. I felt alive again and ready to carry out whatever assignments I was given.

After healing up quite fast and gaining most of my weight back, I often wondered what it was they gave me that night. Some kind of shots that did wonders for my physical and mental health. I suppose the government has drugs that are not on the market that maybe they only give certain people. I was lucky to be part of that group.

I received a phone call and was told to fly into a certain area of the US. Upon my arrival, they picked me up and were totally different than before. Very nice and talkative. I guess I passed the test and now was in their organization, which made me feel like part of a team even more.

There were no more blackout drugs, no more "cover your head"—nothing—I was in. We drove to the desert, where I could see nothing really but some old buildings and sand. I was a little confused but didn't feel threatened at all. I was in the group and probably a very small group and was ready for training.

I got out of the SUV and was escorted to the side of the mountain. The mountain just looked like a mountain to me, nothing special. But in a few it opened up, and there was a huge tunnel with a golf cart waiting on us. I was told to climb in and have fun.

After a few hundred yards, the tunnel widened, and I was inside one of those secret places the government has. I won't go into a lot of detail, for good reasons, of course, but I can tell you that it was truly amazing, and I had never even seen anything like this before. It was a work of art.

I was escorted to a room where I met a guy dressed in normal clothing who had a very hard look about him. His aura was very red if there was one. I could tell this guy was no nonsense. He was sitting there eating and offered me some food. I agreed and sat down with him, while everyone else left the room.

He told me that he had looked at my file and thought I was a great candidate for this particular program. He thought I was exceptional in my skills and would follow orders without question. I nodded in agreement. He then stated that only a very few get selected for these types of jobs and that I should consider it a very high honor. "The country does not have any idea about us in this capacity," he said, "and they do not ever need to know. The straight fact is our people need us, and they are good with being in the dark. They all think stuff like this goes on but like the idea that they don't really know. Do you understand?"

I nodded in agreement.

"We sometimes are called upon to do horrible things in the name of safety for our citizens," he went on. "We protect our military because they live by a different code of ethics. Also, they are young and would not understand how we operate. We operate under a different code, and we have basically no rules. We are what the public believes as above the law. Which we are. However, we do work under them and must live in silence. The people and military are best to leave out of your daily conversation. You are now no one. You will never be affiliated with any agency; you will never be known as anything but a normal person in society. Only a very select group will know who you are and what you do. You are alone in this world as of today. Your only grace is we know who you are."

He went on to say, "This is a lot to understand, and I get that. You are used to being part of something, and you are. But you have to understand that secrecy is our only way of survival in this world. You will be given many assignments in your career, and you will be paid handsomely for your work and skill set. Know that without people like you, our way of life will no longer exist.

"I am sorry if you thought you were being tested for something else, but this is the path we choose for you. This is a very small path, and you are not alone. There will be missions when you will come across others like you. Even then you will never be able to converse about your life. You are alone in your own head. Only you will know what you are. You will have to be strong and know that your country needs you whether they know it or not. You are their only hope for their way of life. Sometimes the ones behind the scenes get no recognition, but that is the way it's been done and will always be done.

"I just want you to know that if you choose right now that this isn't for you, you will be escorted out, and that will be it. However, if you choose to move forward, then we expect you to be fully on board with this and never question anything again."

I told him I was on board and would comply with what was asked of me. "I want to be part of the team and help my country and people," I said. "I love the idea of all of this. As far as saying anything, I am one of those that don't have many friends anyway and can keep things to myself. I am good to go."

"Great!" he said. "For the next month, we will be teaching you many things. You will learn deadly combat fighting techniques; you will learn torture techniques."

I stopped him and asked, "What does that mean?"

"We don't have time to extract information sometimes," he explained. So we have to do hard techniques in order to gain information quickly, and some of those are extremely deadly and painful. We will get into that shortly." He then told me they would teach me techniques to blend into environments. Basically, camouflage at a new level. "We will also teach you how to read people to know if they are telling you the truth; you must be able to know if the information is correct or not. We will teach you what to do if captured and what to do if tortured. You will be trained like never before. The military has done the basics for you, but we will expand to completely different levels. How do you feel about that?" he asked.

I agreed and asked when we would start.

"Tomorrow morning," he said.

After the conversation ended, I was led to my room and given some books to read. He said, "Over the next month, the books will give you guidance and let you know what to expect each day of training." He then told me this would be my room for the entire time and that I was never to leave without an escort.

The room was totally amazing. It had this big screen that played videos with relaxing backgrounds of my choice: waterfalls, mountain scenes, snow scenes, desert scenes, ocean scenes. I could pick the sounds to go with the backgrounds. I guess because I was in the mountains, they had to make it relax. I had a fridge with an assortment of foods and drinks. I also had a nice couch and a TV with movies I could watch. This was really a deluxe room. Very unique but very awesome. They made me feel at home. They really took care of me.

The next day I was escorted to a TV room with two chairs: one for the instructor and the other for me. He came in and told me that we were going to watch a series of actual torture techniques that had been used and were very effective in extracting information. He said that after each scene we would stop and talk about why they worked and when to use them. I nodded my head and couldn't wait to see this.

I do want to make one thing clear. I will not talk about all the techniques that were taught to me, nor will I disclose a lot of the information. However, I will give you some insight into them and why they are used.

The first technique that caught my attention involved a man who was tied to a chair and gagged. I could hear the other man speaking in a language that I will not specify. I never saw the torturer's face either. My instructor told me that some people are very devout, whether it's to their god or their organization. They will not talk unless you can convince them that enduring pain is worse than being honorable. This is what we do to extract information in a short period of time.

My instructor explained what the torturer was asking the man. He was asking about how many men were inside this particular place. If the man told him, that would be it. However, if he didn't, he was going to take his knife and cut the captive in the thigh to expose his leg bone so he could see it. And then if the man didn't talk to him, he was going to spray lighter fluid on his open wound and then light it. I thought that was really barbaric.

I could see that the man looked afraid, but when the gag was taken out, he still refused to say anything. The man put the gag in his mouth and began cutting his thigh open from his hip to his knee and all the way to the femur. The pain this guy must have felt was beyond my comprehension. The torturer was just as relaxed as if he was cutting butter; he showed no real emotion, nothing.

After the man was done yelling and falling in and out of consciousness, the torturer asked if he would like to talk. The man still refused. I saw the torturer take out a syringe and squirt it into his open wound and light it on fire. WOW, that had to hurt! The man looked as though he was blacking in and out of consciousness. After a minute the torturer tied up the man's muscles and put out the fire using both muscles to smother the fire. That is one way to stop the bleeding, I guess.

After the man calmed down, the torturer removed the gag and told his captive that he was going to do the same thing on the other leg. He told the man, "I don't even think you're ready to talk, so I will just do it anyway." The man begged continually until the torturer listened to everything the man was giving up. The torturer got all the intel he needed and was convinced it was the truth and then reached over and slit the man's throat. Again, like it was nothing.

My instructor asked me what I thought of this technique. I agreed that some people will not talk unless you put them through so much pain that nothing else matters but to tell everything they can to get the torture to stop.

He said, "Exactly." He then went on to explain the proper way of cutting the thigh open to not hit the artery. It was like flaying a fish. He asked me if I had to do this to help our country out of a possible terrorist attack whether I'd be capable.

"Absolutely," I said.

He told me, "Good, because you will get your chance."

The next video was of a man of a different nationality that they needed some information from. Again, he was tied up and gagged. This time the man was trying to tell them things, but for some reason the torturer didn't believe him. So, the torturer took out a big syringe and told the man that he was going to stick it in his eye and suck out the fluid, causing blindness.

I thought, Holy hell this is wicked! I asked the guy why he didn't believe the man.

My instructor told me that the torturer had inside intel, and it wasn't matching up with the man's story. OK, I thought. So the torturer stuck in the needle and sucked out the fluid. The man was screaming, even though there was no pain, just screaming because of the loss of sight. What a head game this was.

After the torturer calmed the guy down and squirted his eye fluid onto him, he said the other eye was next. The man started telling him everything and you could just tell he wasn't lying at all. The torturer kept asking more questions, and sometimes the guy really probably didn't know, but the torturer would just stab him a little in the leg or slice a nice cut down his chest. The man was in so much pain he was telling everything, and the story never really changed. Then the torturer just cut his throat.

I sat there and thought, These people do not play; they mean business when it comes to extracting information.

Not only do they use psychological head games, but they match it with pain.

The instructor asked me about this type of torture. I said, "Losing sight is a big thing to people, That was a really good way to get them to talk, and spraying them with their own eye fluid must really mess with them. Then just making cuts to them like it was nothing, you would begin to feel that this person isn't playing nor playing by the rules. It's impressive, for sure."

The next video was disturbing to me. It began with the same scenario: a guy gagged and tied to a chair, just sitting there. The torturer was talking in another language and then did the most horrific thing I had ever seen in my life. He cut open the scalp around the captive's head and started pulling down his skin right to his eyes. Wow, this was bad. Then the torturer showed the man a mirror so he could see it. Now that was a head game.

The torturer again was asking the man for information. He still refused to talk even after that scalping. But then the torturer pulled the skin over the man's eyes and nose and then showed him his face. That was at a different level. I can't even explain my own thoughts at that point. The captive was now talking like a rambling idiot. He couldn't even shut up telling everything. I guess that worked, I thought.

Again, the instructor asked me about that technique. I told him I had never even heard of doing such a thing to someone and to show him in the mirror? What a head case that was. I told him I hope that guys never torture me.

MONSTER

The next video was one that was interesting. Again, the man was sitting there tied up. My instructor told me this was a different kind of torture that you will be privileged to use. It involves using everyday chemicals that you can buy that will have a strong effect on making people talk.

The torturer injected the man in his vein with something that clearly caused extreme pain. I could see the tears coming out; the pain must have been extensive. Not sure what the torturer put in there, but it looked unbearable. The torturer told him that was just a little; the next would be more, and the next would be even more. Basically, it burns you inside out. All your veins' arteries just burn and collapse, and you die. But you die in extreme pain.

He then injected one more dose in the other arm and the man was in incubating pain, trying to tell the man to stop and screaming he would tell him anything he wanted, just no more. So it appears that whatever that was worked quite well. The torturer didn't use any more and just cut the man's throat again. I guess he didn't want to waste his liquid death in case he needed it later.

I watched and watched several more techniques over the next few days, and yes, they were all performed on people live. I guess they needed to show me they worked. There was no doubt that these techniques had been used many times and they were masters of what they do. My instructor went into fine detail about why we use certain ones for certain individuals and not others, which I found interesting. The gist was that some didn't talk using some techniques while others did. It was a brutal few days in there.

The next morning after a few days in the TV room, I was escorted to a different type of room. This room was definitely a torture chamber. I won't go into detail much, but I can tell you they had some kind of terrorists in there from different parts of the world, so I was told, and it was my turn to learn how to do these techniques for real.

I performed five different random torture techniques and showed how to do them properly. These people that were being tortured were not giving up information; they were there solely for my training. All I knew was they were very bad people, and why waste a death if we could get some training out of them? I agreed and did what was asked without too many issues. I was a good soldier or whatever I was. Anyway, after several days of torturing people, I passed to the next stage in training.

For some reason I was given a day off to relax and think, I guess. Who knows why they do the things they do. But one thing was for sure: the three meals they brought me were fantastic. I just lay around and read and listened to the ocean and flipped through the scenes. It was very relaxing after the last week.

I was woken up for the next stage of training. This was hand-to-hand and weapons training. Which was right up my alley, I thought. I'd been through lots of that in the military.

I was taken to a room with a guy who was ugly and cut up. I think he'd had one too many fights but was probably the guy to train me. The first thing we did was just fight. He walked up and said, "Defend yourself." He appeared to be taking it easy on me at first, and so was I. I was not really sure what I was supposed to do, really fight or just guard.

It wasn't long before the fight was for my life. He was beating the shit out of me. I had all I could do to try and block him; he was getting more and more brutal with me. Now I realized it was a fight. I did everything I could to beat him, but he simply beat the shit out of me, and I mean beat the shit out of me.

I could tell this guy could have killed me several times if he wanted to. He was no cage fighter like on TV; he was a brutal killer. After he'd beaten me half to death, he sat me down and talked to me about what had happened and why.

He told me that he'd said defend myself and fight. But he knew I wasn't really into the fight. Why not? I told him I wasn't sure what we were really doing. He said, "You have to fight as if you're going to die every time you get into a fight. Fight as if your life depends on it. Tomorrow your life does. Go get cleaned up and rest."

That night I was thinking about what he said and how I needed to just go in and throw down. I thought about this a lot and figured out OK—as soon as I go in, I am just going to go at it and not say anything. I am not sure if I can catch him off guard, but it's my only chance in beating this guy. I am going to punch his solar plexus to try and knock the air out of him and then kick the shit out of this guy. Well, try to.

That next morning, I woke up and was really sore from being beaten up. Normal, I guess. I ate breakfast, and then they escorted me to the room where he was. He was talking to me about how I felt. I casually walked over to him without giving *any signs of attack*. I hit him in the solar plexus, and he backed up and then came at me like a lion. The fight was brutal, and he beat the ever-loving shit out of me even worse this time. I tried everything I could to hurt him, and he never stopped, nor did I. I was still on the ground trying to get up after being brutally beaten. He just laughed at me and told me to stay put. I called him all kinds of names and told him I was fine and asked if that was all he had. I expected more. Of course, not the right thing to say after being knocked completely out. I woke up in the hospital bed and felt like I'd had the holy shit kicked out of me. I don't think I ever felt that beat up in my whole life.

He came strolling in like another day and said, "Good job today. You caught me off guard; that was good. First one to ever do that. See you in the morning."

All I knew is if the fight was tomorrow, I would not stand a chance. I was beaten up pretty badly.

Finally, I went back to my room and couldn't even go to the bathroom. I was in a lot of pain. I woke up in even more pain and figured, OK, today we start training. He showed me I was nothing to him, so maybe he will teach me his fighting techniques.

I stepped into the room, or should I say barely made it to the room. He looked at me and said, "You are ready to go to round three."

I looked at him with my eyes half-swollen shut and thought, Oh fuck, not again. I looked at him and said, "I hope you're ready for the hospital room today because that is where you're going to wake up."

I don't really remember a whole lot of that fight, just that it was over before I closed my mouth again. I woke up in my room and realized I should just shut my fucking mouth.

The next morning, I knew what was coming and that I had no chance, but what do you do? Then I realized he is trying to make me quit, maybe to see if I am a quitter. OK, I am not going to quit, just take another ass whipping, I guess.

I was escorted to the room again, and there he was eating a sandwich, and he just looked at me. He said, "I thought you would try one of your sneaky-ass moves and hit me while I am eating, or are you done now?"

I told him I was rested and ready for another round if he could take it. "However, if you want to quit, I will let you," I said.

He laughed at me and said, "Hell no, I enjoy the combativeness."

I thought, Holy hell, not again; please be joking.

He told me to get ready. I just thought, Oh no, not again please. He danced around and laughed at me. I did try and take a few swings, which were not even close. Of course I couldn't even see. He then proceeded to hit me everywhere, and I was on the ground trying to breathe. He then got on top of me and started to degrade me by giving me a head rub and telling me, "Honey will be alight like a baby." Even though I was completely helpless, I tried to act mad but couldn't do anything. He said, "It's time for another beating, dear." It was the last thing I remembered again.

I woke back up in bed and was completely beat to shit. I was out of options now. I just couldn't take another beating. The man was just too good, and I was in rough shape. I was waiting for the door tap to go, but it never came that day. I guess I was getting a day to rest.

Next day came and the door came open, and I was escorted to the room. He told me this time if I didn't try, he was just going to kill me. I could see in his eyes he was pissed about something—maybe his mother didn't nurse him enough—but evil was in his eyes, and I honestly thought, Fuck, he going to kill me. I gathered up all the strength I could, and we went at it. I even got a few blows in, and he hit me several times. It was almost like the second day. I was putting up a good fight. I was fighting for my life, and he was knocking the shit out of me. This time was different, though; I never quit. I actually thought he was going to kill me. I remember biting his finger trying to bite it completely off before I felt a hammer fist in my jaw. This was a fight. Then he said "Quit" just like that. Done.

He said that was a good fight, better than the others. Now you know what it's like to fight for your life. Anything you can do to win is the answer. Go to your room and rest up, the training starts tomorrow. Wow, I was done with getting beat up. Didn't realize what kind of brainwashing techniques he was using, but it worked.

There was no more quitting now. I understood what he meant. Even though I didn't really quit, I did in the fights before. I got it now.

The next day, even though I was beat to shit, I knew I'd survived the most brutal man in my life. This guy was a master of death. He would kill any of those on TV who thought they were tough; he was the master.

I walked in, and he was ready. We went through several hand-to-hand moves and kill punches. He was unbelievable in his training. I never even had a clue you could kill someone so easily with your hands. TV had nothing on this stuff. This man knew every inch of your body and what it meant to hit. For the next few weeks, we trained day in and day out.

Although the fighting techniques were very brutal, he was very careful not to hurt me. He made me train on him time and time again and would ask me, "What does that do? Why do you punch there?" and so forth. It was top notch and not taught anywhere in the martial art world that I know of. His style of fighting was not kicks or anything fancy; it was just killing shots every damn time. Every hold, every move you were dead! If not dead, you wished you were. I never in my life knew this kind of combat. But it was surreal.

My next lesson was being a chameleon. The guy who taught this was something else. It seemed like he could just disappear and show up somewhere else. A very unique and very weird guy.

I was escorted to a room with dummies and walls all around me. My first thought was what the hell was this?

I will not go into this in too much detail because of the secrecy of these techniques, and I don't care to share. But I can tell you a few things. He would walk behind a dummy and then be gone. Then he'd show up somewhere else. Truly amazing.

One of the techniques involved disappearing into a room full of people. If someone is watching you or following you, you must get something between you both such as a pillar and another person. Instead of walking to the side as if you are coming behind the person, you walk straight back, keeping the object between you both, if that makes sense.

Our minds play tricks on us, and when we expect something and it doesn't happen like we think it will, we get confused. This is why this technique is so used a lot. I hope that my instructions help, not confuse you more. It's just a trick to be used when trying to lose a tail.

The next trick he showed me was using walls and objects to break up your outline of being a person. I kind of knew this from being a sniper but just in a different way. We would walk into a tunnel, and he would suck up into a wall and show me how hard it was to distinguish him from another end. I would walk down and look back at him. Now mind you, I knew he was there, but if I hadn't, he would have been easily missed. He always told me to become the object that you are attached to. Whatever that meant.

We practiced these two techniques quite a lot, and after a while I could see how someone could disappear right before me. I really enjoyed his lessons on different dodging techniques. We spent time being followed and the strategies for changing directions and then coming back around and all kinds of nifty little tricks. He emphasized several times how the human mind works and how it can be manipulated. When the mind is expecting something, and it doesn't happen, then it gets confused for a split second, and that is your time.

Then we went into blending in with a crowd, even of people from different ethnic groups. He talked about and showed me movies and asked me to pick out his guy. Couldn't do it. Basically, you must never wear anything that would draw attention to you. Look like you are bored and never stand on the side of the crowd or in the front or back. Casually engage in conversations about anything like you know the person.

Also, he stressed that you should have no distinct marks such as tattoos, beautiful eyes, or some logo on a hat or shirt. You want nothing so there is nothing to distinguish you from anyone else. You need to look boring and inconspicuous.

I knew that his advice about fitting in with a crowd was right on the money. Don't walk a certain way, no fast movements of any kind. (Fast movements are seen out of your peripheral vision and can cause someone to look in your direction.) Always avoid eye contact; you should act like you are just there. He told me that you can see everything if you learn to just look without looking. In other words, you don't have to make eye contact to see someone's face. Notice what they are wearing, how they walk, who they are walking with, and so forth. Once you notice what you are looking for, the rest is easy. For example, I might be watching someone who is continually looking for someone like me. Look at what they are wearing and how many are around them. You can keep boring your ass around and nonchalantly keep track of them without the eye contact. Once you make eye contact, they have you. Never look at their face.

The best advice he gave me overall was to look normal and like everyone else. Do not overdress; do not do anything that makes you different. He was a true master of hiding in a crowd or disappearing. As long as you understand how the mind works and how people think and expect, it's easy to manipulate and move and disappear.

We played a game called KIM. Keep it in memory. We would walk through places, and he would ask me what I saw. It was tough at first, but I did this in the military as well. After a while it was easy, like you noticed anything, especially if it was out of character. You would just make a note in your head of what you saw with just a glance and try and remember it. It just takes practice, and you can perform this task easily.

I spent the next four days or so going over this observation method with him. Practice and practice; it is truly a neat way of looking and seeing. Once you realize what you are looking for, it is easier for you to disappear or for you to find someone looking for you. You become more aware of your surroundings.

The next few weeks were full of teaching. We spent a few days on different countries' weapons and everything I needed to know about them. I now know why because those weapons were the ones issued to me in the missions. I guess using other countries' weapons and not American weapons confuses the enemy as to who you are and who you work for. Smart techniques.

We spent a few days on bombs and how to make them with anything really. That was extremely interesting. I really didn't know you could make bombs out of things around the house. I also didn't know you could make toxic substances either. There are so many things that were taught to me over that month that I had no idea even existed. These guys are truly the masters of everything, and they are the ones that protect our way of life. I felt very privileged to be part of this group.

They were all there to give me one-on-one attention to help make me what I became: a monster. I also know they gave me lots of drugs of some sort. They told me it was to help with my health because of the areas I would go to. Not sure what was in these drugs, but I have to say I felt great and alive.

They also informed me of what was to come. They told me I would have a normal life but would be called at any time to perform my duties. Also, if the job was too big, they would have someone like me to assist. It was up to us to secure the job and finish the missions. It was also very important that we never talked to each other about our personal lives. We were never there, we didn't work for anyone, we were there to assist the other, and that was all.

They emphasized this many times to me. They told me it was for my own safety and that they were the only ones who knew who I was, and that was it. I was basically on my own to save the world. That was how I took it anyway. They had my back and knew where I was every minute of the day. They also told me I would never see any of these people who trained me ever again. They didn't exist.

As far as anyone else was concerned, I would be just another guy blending in the work field and trying to make a living. I would be alone in this life. This life is horrible and without recognition. I am a secret to the American public, but yet I am there to protect them even if they don't know it or ever thank me. I am their protector.

He then went on and asked me how I felt and if I had any questions. I really didn't know what to think, so I just said, "I am good."

He reiterated that the American people need people like me. "You are their only hope," he said. "Remember that. Even when you do missions that seem horrible, it is for a reason, even if you don't understand why. Remember we are here for you always, and we see everything. You will always have the best gear, the most intel that we can provide. These missions should be cut and dry."

He then stood up and shook my hand. "I really wish you all the best to come and hope you enjoy protecting your family and our way of life. We will be in touch with you shortly. Remember secrecy is our way of life."

That was it, and the war had started with me and the immoral people of the world.

One last note: They have a cure for cancer, and it's right under everyone's noses. But even if I told you, you're so brainwashed by the pharmaceutical companies and government you wouldn't even believe me. I have already saved lots of people. Isn't that interesting?

Chapter 9

MEETING ONE OF ME

I spent many a mission with just myself going in and taking someone or a group out. Not a hard thing to do if you have all the intel and element of surprise. The missions were always under twenty people or so, not too difficult anyway. However, one day I was assigned a mission that would take a different toll. I was about to meet a monster just like me.

The usual call came in and told me this mission was going to be a difficult one. They were not exactly sure of the number of terrorists, the place where the event was going to occur was difficult to gain access to, and they were not sure what was inside for personnel. However, they were going to send in help with me on this mission.

This time they instructed me that this mission was critical because of the weapon stash that needed to be recovered for the safety of Americans and because we had to complete the assignment with no personnel alive in the compound. They also wanted a detailed map of our progress and where to find the weapons to be picked up.

The caller also instructed me that this was not a social meeting with my partner; it was strictly business, and no personal information was to be shared by either party. It was best for both of our safety. I supposed if one of us was taken out and the other tortured, we could give away our secrets of hiding undercover in certain jobs we performed in our daily lives. Also, he emphasized that we were not to be taken alive on this one. There would be no outside help, and dying would be our best option if it came to that.

He asked me again if I understood the importance of everything he'd told me. I told him of course, that I understand everything, and secrecy will stay with me. I also said, "Don't worry about me being taken alive. I understand the kinds of tortures that would be done to me, and death would be much better."

He went on to tell me that these types of individuals that we were going to encounter were very religious and very dedicated to their cause. At that point I knew what I was dealing with. I also knew who I was dealing with and that this mission was going to be difficult to accomplish. But again, I liked having missions that were difficult and had a bleak outcome. It excited me and gave me a complete rush. Also, I was excited to meet another monster and have help. This was going to be fun, I thought.

I flew into an airport and was met by one of the men on the ground. He told me that we were going to a safe house where the plans were going to be laid out for us both and that we needed to make our plans to complete the mission. This really struck my interest. It must have been a big one for the government if they were sending two of us hideous bastards in to kill everyone and if not take our own lives. This was like no other mission that I have done up to this point. WOW, couldn't wait.

I arrived at the safe house with another ugly SOB. I'll call him Monster One. I could feel the adrenaline and red aura coming off him. This man looked mean and ready to kill. He was big like I was and full of hate just like me. We were a hell of a pair, to say the least. He shook my hand and said, "Good to be meet you and to work with you on this mission." I said the same back to him.

It's a funny thing. While we sat down with our local adviser, Monster One and I kept making eye contact with each other. I really didn't know how to take that. I wondered if he was there to take me out after the mission. Maybe this is how they retire us, I thought. Not sure, but I think he thought the same. So, as you can guess, we were both on our toes and didn't say a whole lot to each other over the next few days.

We were given the usual intel about the mission and place of action. This was a small compound in the desert with many armed personnel. They also told us that there were many underground tunnels leading from one building to the other. They were not sure where the weapons were stashed but assumed underground somewhere in the tunnels.

He advised us that we would have a local driver who was paid asset to them, and he would escort us around the area and do anything we asked. After the completion of the mission, we needed to take him out for reasons. In other words, we needed to make sure there were no loose links about who did this and why. We both agreed to this and didn't really care about just another person who needed to die. Of course, we didn't want to be exposed either. So easy peasy.

Monster One and I were given all kinds of surveillance videos to study. We studied the maps and looked for entry points and personnel outside. The hardest thing about the mission was the openness of the compound and the difficulties approaching it. They could see us for miles coming in. We had to gain access to the compound somehow, and once we were in, then the killing could start. But we needed to be as secretive as possible and not start an open gunfight.

We made a plan to watch the cars coming in and out and then capture a few of these people and see what they could tell us about inside. Of course, you know what that meant. Torture of course. It would be OK; I was well versed by this time in that aspect.

We had requested some tranquilizer darts to knock out the two or three personnel we captured, and we needed a van of sorts and also a place where we could interrogate them and inflict pain without the yelling being overheard. Our point of contact marked a place on the map just for that type of situation. Good; one point down.

Also, we were going to need clothing that fit into the environment. We did not want to stick out like sore thumbs. Then we requested silencers for pistols and ARs and of course lots of ammo. We also needed certain tools for our people. We needed a nice razor scalper, a few knives, lighter fluid, and few syringes of chemicals to burn them inside out. Our counterpart said they had all of that ready.

After that was all taken care of, we had to come up with a point of observation for a day or two just to see the land for ourselves. Our point of contact was going to drive us around. We made sure that he knew of the place where we were going to take the prisoners; we needed to make sure that he knew how to take us around without attracting attention. Apparently, he knew the area quite well and was good to go.

While sitting there with Monster One, we talked about the entire mission and the best course of action. We were definitely on the same page, and really, I was glad he was there with me. He was a smart guy with lots of ideas. I asked him about the point of entry and what he thought was the best way. I suggested that we go through the front gate in a car or just sneak in over the wall at night. They were the only two options. If we came in through the gate, we could very easily start an all-out gunfight that neither of us wanted. So we decided to make our way to the west end of the building, where it was less fortified.

Then I asked him, "Do we stay together, or do we separate and just each take a building and clean house?" Either one was fine with me. I had been doing this for so long that I was used to working alone. But still I wanted his insight. He thought the best option was to go in together because we could have a better chance if caught and discovered. At least we could cover each other's backs better than being alone. I told him that would be fine with me, too, if he didn't shoot me in the back. Now that caused a weird look from him. He didn't even say anything. He was probably thinking the same thing. I was just trying to get a laugh out of the guy, but I guess he was a no-nonsense kind of guy, strictly business. OK, I could do that as well, even though I always tried to find humor in this crap. I guess it helped me deal with it better. Apparently not him.

Everything was in order for the mission now. Now, of course, it was time for our shots. Again, I have no idea what they always gave us before a mission, but I can relay this. We were very aware of everything, on high alert times ten. We had aggression and felt invincible. To be honest, I loved these routine shots that we were told were only for disease control. Yeah, right, I thought. I knew they were something totally different; they made us supermen. Yes, that could all have been in our heads, too, because of the usual adrenaline rush before a mission, but it just felt like something else. It's hard to explain, but the next day was no nonsense; we were out to kill and accomplish.

Chapter 10

OBSERVATION

We made our escort take us to the place of submission first to see what we were dealing with. It was a nice shack in the middle of the desert. No one would hear the screams from here, I thought. We set up our tools of the trade and placed everything in order.

Next, we asked him to take us to a place where we could see the compound and not be noticed. He said he knew just the right place. He was correct; we were out of sight and could observe everything. We both had spotting scopes and took lots of notes to compare later. We watched a few cars coming in and out. We assumed they were going into town for supplies or whatnot. That was great for us; we just needed to know where they were going and the best place for our rendezvous.

We asked our driver what he thought, and he didn't have any idea, of course. That was all right. We then asked him where we could intersect the cars so we could take the people with us. He showed us a location on the map that looked like a good place of attack. Although he was helping us, I didn't really trust the guy not to throw us under the bus. I told Monster One, "After we get to the shack, let's finish him off. We can drive ourselves to the compound."

He looked at me and said, "Yes, I agree with that. I don't trust him not to sell us out either."

Good. Done.

I also told Monster One, "I think we need to do this now and go grab them so our driver doesn't have a change of heart. We also need to take the cars they are driving to the shack."

He agreed.

"After we dart them and get them in our car," I said, "I will take their car and follow them."

We told the driver that we were going to go and cut off the next car that left the compound. Just like I thought he would, he said, "We could do it tomorrow if we wanted to."

This kind of confirmed I really didn't like him and that we would be set up. Not going down this road, I thought. I said, "No we will go to the next car."

"OK," the driver said.

Now, maybe he was nervous or what I don't know, but this was our mission, and he was a liability. I was not going to end up dead because he didn't want to do something when we specified it. No way!

After about an hour or so, we noticed three individuals getting into a truck and were nicely packed for the taken. I told Monster One, "This is it. Let's go."

We got up and told the driver to take us to the point of attack. I felt something was off about him, like he'd sold us out. Maybe our contact was right about killing him too. I thought to myself, Better make sure and just torture his ass to see if he told them anything. I relayed this to Monster One, and he said he was thinking the same damn thing, and yes, we would soon find out with all four of them. I was pleased we were on the same page. I guess since both of us were trained by the same outfit, it proved to me that we were robots and thought alike.

We arrived earlier than the car because we had a much shorter ride than they did to the point of attack. We popped up the hood and looked like everyone else in the country. We told our driver to get off in the road and flag them down, which he did.

We slowly walked up to the truck while our driver was talking to them and shot them all with the tranquilizer guns. They went out fast. I thought to myself, This is just too easy. That did bother me, but again these were just everyday so-called soldiers. In reality, they shouldn't have stopped, but apparently they didn't see any threat either. Either way they were moved into the van, and I proceeded to follow them in their truck.

We finally arrived at the shack!

Chapter 11

TALK TIME

We had four chairs in the room, but there were six of us including the driver. After we tied the three soldiers up, Monster One looked over at me and then shot the driver with a dart as well. The driver looked surprised to say the least. I kind of laughed and said, "He didn't see that coming, did he?"

Monster One said, "Nope, I guess, not."

Then the funniest thing came out of Monster One: "Well, they are waking up here in a few. You like white or dark meat?"

I laughed and said, "I can really go either way."

He asked me to come outside to discuss our thoughts on how to proceed. I told him, "We could do all three while the driver watches. Start on one and let the other two watch, and then start on number two and so forth so they can all watch each other suffer. Or we can do them all separate, which would probably be the best way to make sure we are getting the same stories. Either way I am fine with whatever."

He agreed that if they were separated would probably be the best, but certainly if they watched the others, they might be more inclined to speak up too.

Then I said, "Let's take one in the one room to do and just let the others hear him scream, and then when we are done, drag him out for the others to see. Mess with their minds and maybe get better information."

He agreed.

When we went back into the room, they were all a little drowsy, and we told them what to expect and if they wanted to tell us now, it would save them time of being tortured. Of course, they just cursed us. Of course. they were getting it anyway; we just thought they might want a the come to Jesus chat first. They were praying to their God, and that excited us both even more.

Monster One dragged one soldier into the back room. This one seemed to be the ringleader telling the others all kinds of crazy shit. I told Monster One, "I would really like to do this one myself. He just pisses me off for some reason."

He said, "By all means, help yourself."

I wanted to do the really nice torture first. I wanted to do the leg and let him burn a little and cut open the thigh. But then I had an epiphany hit me. I started in on his right wrist and cut through the wrist and took his hand off. There is a reason I took the right hand off but I'll get to that later. I then sprayed his wrist with lighter fluid and watched it burn. I can tell you the smell was something else. I really enjoyed his pain. It felt so good.

After an hour or so, I let him recover and then told him I was going to slice into his thigh and separate his muscles so he could see his leg bone, and then I was going to spray lighter fluid in there to stop the bleeding, and then I was going to do the next leg and then the arms. I also told him I was going to do this over a few days so he could recover from one before the next while I tortured the others, and if he failed to tell me anything that didn't match their stories, I would keep him there until his body was completely mutilated. I could tell he knew I was serious.

He told me nothing. I said, "OK, here we go." I started nicely and slowly cutting into his thigh separating his muscle. He started talking. We asked about tunnels and where the weapons were and what kind. He blabbed on for a little and then shut up. I sprayed the fluid in his leg and lit it on fire and then grabbed two pieces of rope and tied the muscle together to stop the fire. He was screaming so loudly in pain. Then he really started to talk. Anything we asked him, he told us. Told us how many personnel to expect, who was the leader, where he slept, and where weapons were stored. (He had apparently lied before; this was a different place.) So maybe that torture technique worked. Then he told us how we could get in from a different area. That was helpful; we didn't know that one.

I then drugged him out alive so the others could see. They were all muffled and screaming, and he was slightly unconscious. Monster One dragged another in, and he said he would do this one. So, I watched as he told the soldier what to expect from losing his face. His eyes were wide open, and he was talking. After he got done, Monster One made a nice incision around his head for taking off the skin and peeling it down over his face. Really gruesome idea. But hey, whatever works, works.

Monster One asked him the usual questions again, and some of his answers matched the other man's but not exactly. So, he began peeling the man's face past his eyes and then stopped and showed him a mirror so he could see himself. Wow, what an effect on his spirit. The man just started telling us everything, but his answers still didn't quite match everything, but I think we both agreed that he was telling us the truth.

Monster One dragged him out, and I grabbed number three. This man, after seeing the other two, didn't need much convincing; he was telling us everything he knew. Surprisingly enough, his answers matched number two's. But we had to make sure he wasn't hiding anything, so I sat in front of him and explained what I was going to do to him.

I explained that in this little needle was a nice chemical that was going to burn out his veins and arteries and make him wish he was dead. He begged me not to do it, insisting that he was telling the truth. I really did believe him, but hey, had it anyway, so why not?

I injected him in his right hand just a little bit so he could get a taste of it. He screamed so loudly even Monster One and I looked at each other. I said, "Wow, that must hurt." The man started telling us about the same things over and over. Monster One asked if he had ever seen the guy out in the room with them (the driver). I'd forgotten to ask that question. The man said no, he had never seen him before but wasn't sure who he was.

I stuck some more chemical in his left hand, this time a little more than before. The man screamed so loudly he passed out. I told Monster One, "I think he has told us everything, but we should go and bring the first guy back in."

He responded, "It sounds like fun."

When we dragged number three out, the others were mortified with fright. Which was to be expected. The driver was trying like hell to chat with us, but it wasn't his turn yet. We dragged in number one. I told him his stories didn't match up with the other two's, and this time it was going to be bad for him if he didn't start telling the truth. He was in fear, and at this time I don't think his God or cause was in his mind at all, just the torture that was going to happen to him next. In fact, he begged for death, and I told him, "Oh no, we got plenty of time to have fun with you."

He started telling us about the same shit over and over. I got tired of it, so I took out a dental hook and reached in and took his eyeball out of his left eye socket. He screamed, and then I pulled out the optic nerve a little and made him look at his eye with the other. That was a sight. LOL.

That was finally it for him; he told us all we needed to know, and there were no lies from him this time. We dragged him out to the rest of them and then brought the driver into the room and ungagged him.

The driver was begging for his life as usual. Monster One and I had heard this many times. But like always, neither he nor I gave a shit. We told him we knew he'd been talking to them and was going to give us away, but if he told us what he'd said, we would let him live. He told us many times that he didn't ever talk to them and gave us many reasons. Although I kind of believed him, we still had to check.

Monster One said, "I will take care of this one." I stepped back and watched Monster One tell the man he was going to light his feet on fire and let his legs burn off. He said that he would spray fluid on top of his feet so the fire would burn into his legs to the bone. "So now is the time to tell us what you said," Monster One told him.

Gruesome, I thought, but this ought to be good.

The man insisted that he was innocent, but Monster One did as he said, and the man screamed in pain as the flesh was being burned to the bone. As the fire died down, Monster One sprayed more and more. The man never did confess. So, he probably didn't say anything to anyone about us. It was time to end this now.

We dragged him out to the rest of them, and Monster One thanked them for their cooperation. He looked at me and said, "You have anything else?" I told him no, I was good. He nonchalantly walked to each one and cut their throats from one end to the other. That was it; they were all dead, and we got what we needed.

Chapter 12

MISSION TIME

Monster One went out to the truck and gathered the gasoline cans, and then we poured it all over inside. We gathered all our stuff and lit the shack on fire. We also parked the truck right next to it so it would burn up as well. Once the fire was ablaze, we got in the van and left.

We parked in the same area as before so we could observe the compound and ate some food and drank water and just observed for a while. Monster One asked me my thoughts. I told him, "We should go through the hatch on the other side and sneak in through that. The man said it wasn't booby-trapped or anything, just hidden. Then we would have to deal with the men inside, but that shouldn't be much of a problem. We could take out as many as possible from underneath, giving us less chance of a big gunfight up top."

He just looked at me and said, "Let's go tonight about two a.m. and start killing them SOBs.

"OK," I said.

BOB W. CANNADY

We sat there and counted men up top all day and figured there were about twenty-five or so. We were not sure how many were below, but it should be an in-and-out process. I really didn't see it being too difficult. I rather doubted these people ever would believe anyone would come and even try them. Too arrogant. But surprise—monsters are coming for you.

That night we each took our shot to help us become "more adaptable" to anything down there. My ass. It was an aggression shot if anything. My thoughts only. I really and honestly believe they were experimenting, trying to make a perfect killing weapon that could be shot and keep on going. At least I felt invincible. And I liked it!

Two a.m. came, and we were at the hatch entryway. Monster One wanted to lead, and I didn't care. I told him I had his back. He looked at me strange like I was going to shoot him in the back. I told him, "Not that; I will cover your six, big guy. Let's just get this job done and go home." He shook his head at me and opened the hatch very carefully so as not to set off anything.

The man was correct; there were no alarms or bombs, just the escape hatch so the big boys could get away in case the military showed up. Pretty ingenious, I thought. You could not be seen by the compound, which was 150 yards away.

We made our way down with the help of some dim lights that were lit. Monster One walked very slowly, and we had our Chinese Ars with silencers attached to them and a shitload of ammo. We walked for a while and finally heard some noise at the other end of the tunnel.

MONSTER

We stopped and listened for a minute. Sounded like men sleeping. This was a good sound.

We made our way to them and found two of them sound asleep lying on cots. We both reached for our knives and simply cut their throats together in sequence. It was like we were tied to each other's thoughts and didn't have to even say anything to each other. Very weird thing that was.

The tunnel forked, and we knew the weapons were to our left and not straight ahead because that is what the first man had told us. So we looked at each other, and Monster One took the lead to the left. We walked about fifty yards or so and found a nice pile of anti-aircraft missiles, pounds of C-4, piles of AK-47s with ammo, grenades, US 50 cals, type 67-2 machine guns, large quantities of 155 mortar rounds, boxes of RPGs, Soviet 82-pm-41 mortars, and lots more. The room was huge, to say the least, and I could see why our government wanted this stuff. Not sure why they didn't want us to just blow it, but they never did. Their idea was for us to take out everyone and leave. But this mission was slightly different. We had to stay until they showed up and make sure no one else came into the compound after the mission. I guess we were their security for moving this stuff. Never understood that part or why the military wasn't involved, but who cares—we had our orders.

We looked around and didn't see anyone else. So we backtracked after taking an average count of what was there. We went back to the two dead men and went straight. As before, we could hear noises in the background. We proceeded quietly and made our way closer and closer.

When we finally arrived at the next intersection, we found two more guys with radios sound-ass asleep. Again, throat-cutting time. Then we proceeded to the next section where the big cheese was supposed to be. The door was beautiful with some kinds of markings. Not sure what, but this was it for him and his wives.

We opened the door and commenced to shooting everything in sight. I'm not going to go into too much detail, but women and a few men and young men died in that room. None of them even saw us coming. It was fast and silent, and in less than twenty seconds, Monster One and I had killed them all in the beds. None of them even woke up.

We made our way to room after room and corridor after corridor, killing all that we found that night. By now it was around 4 a.m., and we only had a little time left to clear the top buildings.

We made our way to the surface and began clearing each house and room until no one was left. The guards at the front and end were the first to die and then everyone else.

Only one time did we find anyone awake, and he was taking a piss. It was his last. After all was cleared, we pushed our button, and Monster One and I went to the main gate and waited.

After a short while, we saw a car heading our way. This car had one of our guys in there telling us that lots of big trucks were coming in and for us not to fire upon them. That was nice of them, I thought.

They came in with five large trucks and lots of people. They all bailed out, and the one adviser came over to us and had us show him the weapons. Afterward we escorted him down, and he knew where they were. We were asked to stay at the gate and deal with anything that came in. He also told us, "There is no more of us, so anyone else is a bad guy. Deal with them." Enough said.

We sat there, Monster One and I, and watched as they loaded everything up in the trucks. After about an hour or so of them moving everything, we could see dust flying down the road. I looked at him, and said, "I think we have a visitor coming." He agreed, so we quickly changed into our local clothing and sat there.

When the car pulled up, Monster One walked over to them, and I came in from behind and shot them both in the head. I think Monster One was mad at me. I did make a mess, and we had to move the car and neither one of us wanted to get in and drive it now. OK, I got excited; I should have shot them in a different place, I guess. The head does make a mess.

He opened the door and looked at me like "It's your fucking mess; you drive and park the car." I guess I deserved that. I moved the driver's body over to the middle and stuck my head out of the driver's window because the front window was covered in brain matter. I moved the car out of the way and came back. Yes, I had shit all over me. I deserved it, though.

I came back to Monster One and told him, "Next time I do the talking, and you can do the other." He just smirked at me. For some unknown reason, we were starting to get along and connect with each other. But my humor was much better than his; I am one funny SOB in times like this. He wasn't so much. But he was coming around.

No more cars came, so el Monster One wouldn't get dirty, I guessed. Our point of contact told us to leave after the last truck and meet back at the safe house. We both nodded, and he left.

On the drive back to the safe house, I told Monster One, "I am glad they picked you to assist me on this mission."

He looked at me and said, "I am glad *they picked you to assist me on this mission.*"

No use seeing whose dick was bigger; we were both big boys and not used to help. I just laughed and said, "It's nice that you have some kind of humor and aren't just a robot."

Again, he looked at me and smiled. "Pot to kettle."

We made it back to the safe house, and neither one of us killed the other, so that was nice. As I stated earlier, I had not really been sure if he was there to kill me after the mission or if he thought the same. But not this time, just do a job and go home.

We made it back and went our separate ways. I sure would like to have run into him again, but for some strange reason, every time I worked with another monster, it was someone different. Maybe he died or maybe they didn't want us to get close enough to talk. I will never know the reason, but I sure would like to chat with him again.

The only last thing I thought about him was that he was such a mean, big, ugly guy, what kind of job could he possibly have that didn't give him away? It was not like he could be a cookie salesman or anything. Maybe he was a married spouse to an oil field worker and he was the stay-at-home mom. LOL. Good luck, my acquaintance.

Chapter 13

DISTRACTION

One of the many aspects of killing is learning good tricks of the trade and having the right material to pull it off.

You ever sit in a bar or restaurant and see a beautiful woman walk in? It's quite funny; all the men are looking, and the wives and girlfriends are looking at the men staring. The key point is no one is looking anywhere else; they are completely distracted from everything else.

Another example is driving down the highway and seeing an accident on the other side of the freeway, but yet everyone on this side of the freeway slows down although they don't even need to. People want to see what is going on, and they become very distracted. They don't even see anything but what is going on, on the other side of the road. People's brains just focus on distractions.

This is great information for someone like me. Now if people hear a gunshot, they are getting the hell out of the way and don't want to even know what is going on. So with that in mind, monsters like me must use this knowledge to our advantage.

MONSTER

I know if someone's house is on fire, everyone will go, gather together, and watch. They don't feel it's necessary to help but to observe. Likewise, if someone is having a heart attack, they will bunch up to look. Great for me but not for them. This is what this next mission I will describe was all about: how to gather people in one area and make my life easier.

The next time you feel like being distracted could be your last.

Just like all missions that I have done over the course of many years, I received a phone call and was asked to catch a flight to a particular destination. After reaching the destination, it was clear that I was on my own for this one. Which was no big deal—really, that is the way I liked it anyway, unless it was too big for one person, but taking care of fifteen was easy.

I sat down with a map and looked at the groundwork that lay ahead. They had one person they needed me to take out for some reason, and anyone else I could take out would be greatly appreciated. Not a bad gig. Some of the missions were just like that: they wanted one person eliminated. Why, I had no idea, but that is what they asked for and that is what they would get.

This mission was centered on a few small houses in the Middle East area. I thought it would be easy enough to kill the one person; I could just snipe him out. But I had the feeling that they would appreciate it if I cleared the houses and ended all of them.

I studied the map of the house and other little houses around the area. Not really much but very close to the town and not much different from those around the area. I didn't see this guy as much of a big honcho, but I am sure they had their reason. Who was I to ask? Besides, I really liked these little jobs, and I liked the area I was going to because of the security of Americans there. I would not look out of place at all and could easily just dress how I wanted.

I looked at my liaison and asked for C-4 and a detonator. I also asked for a nice bottle of heart attack. (This is a bottle containing certain chemicals that gave you a major heart failure and nothing could save you; just a drop or so in coffee, and it was over. You could also use it on a door handle—very toxic). I also asked for my usual pistol and AR silencer. Just in case.

I asked my driver to show me the place so I could take a look and see what I was dealing with. I also wanted to see the person I was after and learn from his habits. I might need a day or two just to observe him like previous missions. I just didn't want to jump into the mission, even though it was cut and dried and could have been done in an hour. Just never know.

I had the driver drive around the area and just looked for the rest of the day. I didn't see much that was a harm to me. It looked like an easy task that anyone could pull off. I then asked the driver if he would take me back to the liaison. I had a question to ask.

I asked the liaison if the man ever was known for explosives. He told me was affiliated with that and asked why. "If an explosive device went off, would people expect that from him?" I asked. He looked at me and said yes, possibly. That was all I needed to know. It would be very simple.

The next day I asked the driver to take me back to the target's house so I could look. I counted about seven men and a few women and no underage children. This was good for me. Some of the men had weapons and some didn't. I didn't see any military personnel or anyone that resembled them. Just a few guys with guns and nothing more. The job looked easier than before.

I was ready to complete a one-day job and move on to the next adventure. But like I stated, some of the jobs were difficult and some were not. This one was a simple in and out. I just needed to figure out how to poison the man, draw others in, and finish them all with one nice explosion and walk away.

I started with my driver, and he dropped me off at dusk. I knew prayers would soon be coming, and this was my time of attack. Although it was completely unethical to strike during prayer time, it did gather everyone up.

I just had to figure how to get in and set everything up for the attack. After walking around and looking, I decided that I needed to wait for morning prayer. I needed dark to set up everything and be a little more discreet in my actions. Now if I just wanted to kill everyone and make noise, that would be easy, too, but I'd rather be safe. You just never know.

After evening prayer, I saw them gather around to eat and smoke shisha. This would also be a nice time to do what I had to as well. I observed the man I was looking for and saw where he sat and what pipe he used. This would be a good place to put the chemicals in. Although a few might have heart failure, that would be OK too.

When all was done and evening time came, they were finally going to rest around 10:30 p.m. I watched a man wash out the shisha pipes and put them back in the original place of each one's setting. That made me happy. The only problem that I saw was if they didn't do shisha in the morning after breakfast. That could cause a problem for me. But I was not sure how to find out. I should have taken more time to see what they did in the morning and whether this was their ritual or not. If not, then I would have to stay around till evening. That would be no big deal, but this was the port of entry.

Everything was quiet except a few people wandering around town, and I just moseyed around with them like a stupid tourist. I chatted with a few and had some water or tea. Then about midnight I walked to their house like I was just looking around lost. I was not a big concern to anyone at this time. I would just stop and look at the stars and act like a dumbass tourist. No one paid me much mind; some would chat, and some didn't. There weren't a lot of people out at that time. I fit right in.

I walked by their houses and saw nothing. Now was my time. I went in and set up the shisha pipe with nice chemicals for anyone who smoked from it. Then I had a brilliant idea to just do all of them. There were only four pipes, and several could smoke out of each one. However, I didn't, just in case they started smoking at different times. This stuff acted quickly, so I just did the main guy's pipe. I hoped he'd be there at smoking time. I should have done more research, but what the hell. If all else failed, I would just go and ghost his ass anyway.

I then set up enough C-4 to take out everything around for a hundred-foot explosive radius. All around the shisha area and food. They sometimes eat while smoking, so I just wanted to cover all bases. Yes, I decided not to do it at prayer time. I had some ethics in me, but only some, I suppose.

I knew that once he started in on his pipe, he would experience heart failure and all would gather around to try and help. This was the time I planned for the C-4 to detonate, trying to get as many as possible. If some didn't get killed, then they were the lucky ones. I was not going in and taking them out. He was the main target, and the other ones were just a bonus.

After morning prayer, they all went and ate and sat around and talked; then they went over to the shisha area to lie on soft mats and smoke and chat. It wasn't long before the shisha was lit, and my target was sitting there waiting to puff. There were also three others joining him on his pipe as well. Four heart failures coming up.

It didn't take long for everyone to start puffing away while I sat and waited for his turn to be lit. Good leader that he was, he was last and letting everyone else start first. Hmm, nice of him, I thought.

Then his turn came up, and all four of them were puffing way. I waited for about thirty seconds or so before I could see them moving in a strange position. I could tell that it was coming, and they felt uncomfortable. Not long after that, all four were grasping for their chests. This was as expected, of course.

Also just as I'd expected from previous missions, everyone started gathering. I could see they were blaming the shisha because the chest pains were affecting all four who'd used the same pipe. The nice thing was people were coming out of the house, and more than expected came to aid the four smokers. This was going to be a nice gathering. I hope they get their virgins when they get to heaven, I thought.

The nice thing about setting off the explosion, was people from the town would gather and I could just walk away while they focused their curiosity on the bomb. I would not even be noticed. How easily are people manipulated? They are just sheep, and all have the same behavior. Let's go look and see, even though the one responsible is right here with us, and we don't even notice him. People in a group are just dumb.

It was time to set off explosives and see what happened. I recognized about twenty-three people were there standing around to gawk at the four men. Perfect! I pushed the button and blew shit everywhere. Body parts blew in every direction, and the cloud of smoke went as high as I could see. I was only about sixty yards away behind a small building, and the bombs were massive. I guess I put a little more than needed, but what the hell; it took care of the job.

As expected, people were outside gathering like sheep to see what happened instead of getting the hell out of the area in case more was to follow. A perfect distraction for me to exit. They were running past me and never even paid me any mind. God, I love how people behave.

I walked down the street and just made my way back to the hotel. Of course, I acted as though I was scared and wanted to get the hell out of there. This, of course, would be expected from a tourist. We are just weak, scared little rabbits. If only they knew.

I walked into the hotel, and the staff escorted me to my room, telling me we had a terrorist attack, and I should stay in my room and be safe. I asked them what happened just like anyone would have done to throw off the scent of a predator. They were so nice and accommodating. I love people; they are just so predictable. Hahaha.

I walked into my room and arranged to meet my driver and liaison. Then I left everything there and re-dressed myself to change my appearance and departed for the airport. Another job well done and safe and sound.

The reason why I put this chapter in was to show you how easy it is to manipulate and distract people. What makes them come and see or run like hell. Bullets make them run, but fire, medical emergencies, and explosions make people curious. People like me pray for those who can't see anything but what is happening. It gives us a clear avenue to do our jobs.

Chapter 14

JUNGLE KILLING AND DESTROYING

After the last mission, I was giving the usual time off, which was about three weeks to recover and settle down. Every time we monsters were sent out, they did the same thing. Gave us time off and let us cool down before we went back to work. I guess this was a reset for us.

I always found one thing interesting throughout my missions. They were generally the same: go hunt and destroy the personnel, leave the weapons and drugs found, push the button, and leave. However, the three missions I put in this book were slightly different. One of the missions, we stayed until all were picked up; in another mission no drugs or weapons were involved and we were just sent in to destroy personnel; and in another one, I lost my shit.

This mission was the second one in the pack. We were given orders to just go in and destroy all personnel and leave. There were no drugs or weapons to speak of. My only assessment was that these people had really pissed someone off or were stealing from the wrong group. I guess I will leave that up to you to decide.

As with any other mission, I was given a call, and a plane ticket was ready and picked up at the designated airport. I was escorted to the safe house for a debriefing. When I arrived, I saw a man who was built and looked a lot like me. I knew right away he was a monster as well. I knew then this was going to be a rough one going in. They only sent two of us when they meant business.

I sat down at the table with the man who was our liaison for this mission. He first introduced himself and told us both that we would be working together on this mission and that there were about thirty-plus personnel.

He then told us that all personnel must be eliminated and no one left alive. This was generally the case in every mission, so that wasn't anything new. He also showed us a picture of the man who was the ringleader and said an example had to be made of him for all to see. He was very explicit that this man was to be out front of the compound with only his head.

For some reason, this man had pissed someone off, and an example was to be made. I didn't really care why; it didn't matter to me at all. I just found it strange that we were there to make an example for someone, not to our personnel but to the people of the country.

We had all the intel we needed and lots of great topographical maps of the area. It appeared we would have to trek around in the jungle looking for this guy, which was not an easy task due to the number of personnel we had to take out. They could be anywhere in the jungle. This was going to be a hard insurge and tough to take them all out. For other reasons they would not let us go by road but wanted us to come in from the side. They had their reasons like always.

The liaison looked at us both and said, "You have about a day to look over the maps and come up with your plans, and then we will be back to drop you off."

I will call my new partner Monster Two. Although I worked with a few monsters in my day, they were never the same person I'd worked with on any mission. I guess they didn't want us to get too close to each other. I supposed that made sense. Let us always be in the dark was their motto.

We had plenty of food and drinks in the room for a good session of planning. They usually did supply us with that before any mission. I looked at my partner after our liaison left and said, "Well let's see what we need to do."

The first thing we did was look at the maps and plot our course into the jungle. I supposed intel was telling us that this was the safest route for attack because the other ways were heavily guarded. I supposed this was a nasty hike in and even they wouldn't expect anyone to come in that way.

We marked it out and estimated about a one-to-two day walk in through very tough terrain. This was not going to be easy at all. Looking at the maps, we saw we had several streams to cross and a good fourteen miles in. I can see why they wouldn't expect anyone coming in from this direction. Only two stupid monsters would try this.

MONSTER

After marking out the area, we chatted about where we should camp out each night and also if we got separated where we could have a rally point to meet back up at. We had the four rally points marked on each of our maps and which one to meet at if we separated.

Next was the plan of attack. We knew by intel that thirty-plus were in the village. How could we make sure no one left or made it out? This was going to be the tough part. We had to be quiet and precise in our movements. We had to use knives if we could and silencers if we couldn't.

Once we made it into the village, we decided to go around the outside first and take out anyone guarding the outside parameter. This way we could then work our way closer and closer to the middle. The intel also told us where the big cheese was staying; he had to be last, we decided. This way we could make a strong example out of him for all to see. We were still not sure how to do this, but I had some ideas.

We both sat around and processed the route and how we were going to carry out the mission. We agreed that this was going to be tough and hard. We also had to plan our way out. We both thought we could just drive out and be done. which wasn't that bad of a thought. Why should we track back through the jungle? We were not given instructions on how to leave, so they let us decide that one.

The night went on, and we decided to go to sleep and still ponder our plan tomorrow. For some reason they gave us plenty of time to do this mission. I asked

Monster Two, "What happens if he isn't there? That is always a possibility."

He told me, "We wait until he comes back; the mission isn't done until he is dead."

I agreed with that statement and thought the same thing. We were on the same page for sure about everything.

The next morning, we woke up bright and early and waited for breakfast to be brought in. We ate and sat there looking at the maps and decided to search for the gear they brought us to see if anything was missing.

We went through our goodie bags. We had silent pistols and multiple mags. We also had assault rifles with silencers and multiple mags. Both of us had machetes. We had night vision goggles, knives, compasses, GPSs, batteries, our clothing with two changes of each, paracord, and nice strong wire with two handles so we could wrap it around their throats and silent kill. Also, we were surprised at the amount of C-4 with signal detonators that we could use at any time. Enough to take down the whole village, or better yet, to take out the road coming in.

This time they were not playing with the villagers who were our target; they wanted to ensure these people were all dead. Now with all the new equipment we had to strategize what the C-4 was for and how we could use this for our benefit.

By looking at the map, we realized we could basically blow every building to pieces. As long as we didn't get the main honcho. He was going to be displayed for all to see. I was truly excited about this one.

MONSTER

I told Monster Two my idea was to set all the C-4 with detonators on each building that armed personnel were staying in. Then we would proceed as planned to try and kill all that we could before being noticed. If we were noticed, we would set off buildings and wait for the rest to come out into the open and kill them. Then we would proceed to the honcho's house and take him alive and do what we wanted. He thought this was a decent plan and should take out a lot of them if need be. We didn't want any to escape, and that also meant we needed to disable the cars and trucks.

We talked about the vehicles next. We would have to either flatten the tires or place C-4 at the entryway in case they tried to leave. I then asked if we should stay together or work independently. My thought was we should stay together, take out the outer crews, and then proceed independently to each house. This way we could cover all the houses in a shorter time. He seemed fine with that. Remember, we usually did work alone anyway, so not a big deal. I told him that we should start at the front and work our way back to the honcho's house and then take care of him. But if something went wrong, we would blow the shit out of the place and then deal with him. We agreed.

Our liaison came in and said that we would be dropped off at our point of entry at 0600 in the morning. He gave us our food and water for our rations. He then administered our shots and told us to bed down and get some sleep.

I'm not sure about Monster Two, but I could never sleep the day before. I was always way too amped up. Plus, the shot would send me over the edge with adrenaline (I think). As I stated before, I never really knew what was in the shot, but it always made me feel invincible.

Chapter 15

JUNGLE

The next morning came early. We got up and showered and ate breakfast and were ready to go. Our bags were packed the night before, and the plan was laid out. We each had our own gear such as maps and so forth. In case one did die or was taken out by some unknown reason, the other could finish the mission, even if it was alone. That is what we were trained for, so either way the mission was done and finished, or we both were dead. This could have been a suicide mission because of all the obstacles that lay in front of us. But we were highly trained and eager to please.

We were dropped off on the edge of the jungle, and the vehicle left. We started in the jungle to get out of sight and get our coordinates to our first rally point on the map. We had to go about two miles in for first point.

After we were all suited up and ready to venture, we started off. From this point on, no more communication, just hand signals. We both knew the plan: unless something changes along the way, we stick by it.

We started walking and came across our first swampy stream. We had seen this on the map, so it was no big deal. Monster Two went up one hundred yards and looked for a crossing, and I went one hundred years the other way, and then we would meet back at the same point. This was our plan when we came to a stream.

We both came back, and he signaled to me to follow him. So he took point, and I took the rear. After about fifty yards, he had found an overlying tree that we could make our way over the stream on and them jump off to the next bank. Good crossing.

We had set back out on our course when we heard some noise. We both stopped because we were only in about a mile, if that. We could tell that it was a few men talking. I shook my head and thought we should go around in case they were lookouts. If they were and we took them out, they would be late checking in and give our position away. However, Monster Two wanted to investigate. Our first disagreement. I was not pleased with his call.

We slowly went through the brush until we saw some farmers, I assumed, picking some fruit. I looked at him and shook my head no. He did agree with this, and we backtracked a little and made a circle around them and kept moving in the direction of the next rally point.

We finally made it to the first rally point and sat down for a minute. We double-checked this spot and made sure we were there correctly. We both agreed that this was the place, and this was point one. After that we began our trek to rally point two. Rally point two was five more miles in, and that would either be our camping site or not, depending on how long it took us to get there.

Three miles in, and we were both getting exhausted trying to cut through the brush and zigzagging back and forth. This terrain was heavily wooded and had lots of underbrush. I was glad we hadn't run into any deadly creature so far. I took the lead next and cut and cut for about five hundred yards or so. By this time, I was now exhausted. We were not making much time and still had a long way to go.

I had decided by now I wasn't coming back through this shit. I was driving out. No more two or three days of wearing my old ass out. I was sure if Monster Two could talk, he would be thinking the same damn thing. Again, he was about my age, and we were not spring chickens anymore.

We finally made it to the five-mile mark, and both were exhausted; we still had two more miles to go to rally point two. I looked at him, and he looked at me, and I thought, Fuck this; let's sit for a while and rest up. We both found a nice tree with no snakes around it and sat. We pulled our maps out to check out the terrain ahead of us. He looked up and just frowned and pointed at a bigger stream ahead. I nodded and gave it the finger. He actually almost laughed. Maybe this one had a sense of humor like me.

We sat there for a little while longer and then got up and started off to point two. We had about two hours of daylight. I was not sure if we were going to make it two miles to the point. If not, no big deal; we would find somewhere to bed down for the night and hit it again in the morning.

We were closing in on point two, but the dark was upon us and both of us were tired. So, we bedded down for the night. Not a fun place to bed but good enough. I put my poncho down, too, and my Woobie on top and had my pack for a pillow and off to sleep I went.

I heard something in the middle of the night and looked over to my partner, and he was sitting there looking at me. I raised my hand like "What the fuck was that?" I pointed to my rifle and gave him the hand like "Was that a gunshot?" He kind of shrugged his shoulders and sat there. I sat up to listen as well. About five min or so later, we heard it again, and it was definitely a gunshot. It was in the far distance. I was not really sure how far, but I would estimate by the sound maybe four or five miles away, in the direction we were heading. The shots could be coming from rally point three, I signaled him. He shook his head maybe.

We sat there for another hour or so and heard nothing. I lay back down and motioned to him to get some sleep. We were in the middle of the jungle, and they were far away from us, so we could deal with that in the morning. He agreed with me, lying down, and both of us went back to sleep. No further gunshots. But I was wondering what the hell a gunshot was doing out in the middle of the jungle. Maybe a hunter or something, but yet it was dark. Who would be hunting in the dark?

Daylight came, and I think we were both excited to see what the hell happened last night. So we headed out in our direction to find point two and then make our way to point three. Point three was where I thought the sound came from after I consulted the map. If that was the case, that would put them about three miles or so from the final destination. Again, I was not sure exactly how far they were away, but that was my estimate anyway.

We finally made it to point two. We looked around and sat down and checked out the map. The big stream was right ahead of us. I really didn't want to get wet. But I was not sure we could make it across this one without getting soaked.

We walked to the stream and looked at it; it was nothing short of twenty-five feet across. I gave him the signal to walk up and look for a better crossing, and I would do the same. After a few minutes we were both back, and nothing. This was as good a place as any. We stripped down and put our clothes in the backpacks to stay somewhat dry and waded out into the swampy mess.

We finally made it to the other side of the stream. We were both covered in moss and mud. Not a good feeling but thankfully no leeches. We stood by the banks naked and tried to clean ourselves up before drying off and getting clothed again. I thought this wasn't too bad so far. It actually felt good to clean up.

We started off to point three. The jungle was a mess to trek through, but slowly but surely, we made it to point three. We both did a twenty-five-to-fifty-yard circle around, looking for anything that could have been what they were shooting at, even though it was probably not in this area at all. It's really hard to tell distances in the jungle. But we never saw anything on the way. So, we had one more point to go before contact. This point would be about five hundred yards away from their camp. This way we could make it to the point rather fast if we needed to and regroup.

We kept on walking for a little while. We needed to stop about two miles in and recover and recoup so we could hit the village at night as planned after everyone shut it down. Most of the people would be asleep at night, we figured, and night would also give us good cover and concealment.

We made it to half a mile from our point four. This is where we were going to try and get some rest before going in that night. It was a very well-hidden place and should be safe to crash out for a few hours. We planned on getting up about 11:00 p.m. and then making our way in.

Monster Two and I bedded down and checked all our gear and then looked at the map one last time. Our plan was for the outer to go first and then place the C-4 on certain buildings on each side and then when done start at the front and work our way back. It seemed like a good plan.

The strangest thing happened that evening while we were lying down. We were back to back, looking in opposite directions. This is how we slept so we could cover each other's backs in case they approached from one way or the next. Monster Two said to me in a soft whisper, "My name is Paul."

MONSTER

Wow! I lay there in amazement because we were never ever supposed to do something like that, not ever. After thinking about what he had said I whispered, "Bob."

It was quiet for a while, and then he said, "I am a traveling salesman."

I whispered, "Oil field worker." We both lay there for a little longer. I said, "Montana."

He whispered, "Texas."

I really couldn't believe my ears that this was happening. I spoke up again and said, "Two boys."

He replied, "Four girls."

I said, "Married."

He replied, "Me too, but not happily."

I told him, "I wanted to masturbate; I was horny."

He giggled and said, "I already did last night."

I chuckled and told him he was better looking than my wife.

He snickered and said, "Don't even think it, fucker."

I told him he might need the protein. His body was shaking with giggles, and I said, "Maybe I need some too."

We both had a really good chuckle that evening talking shit before the gunfight and killing started. I knew right off that we could be friends. That evening it was time to start making our way to the point and then to the zone. I grabbed his arm and said, "Bob Cannady from Dillon, Montana, and stuck out my hand.

He grabbed my hand and said, "Paul ?????? from Houston, Texas."

We both nodded at each other. Very weird but I was very happy to finally have a chat with someone like me.

Even though it was forbidden. They were not here on some suicide mission; we were, and it was nice to know the man beside me.

We made our way to point four and put one C-4 by the trail of entry just in case we were followed. We could blow the shit out of them and circle around and finish it.

We crept up to the village and saw the houses just like in the pictures. There were a total of eight houses and a few buildings of sorts. We sat there for some time waiting for everything to quiet down and then to go to bed. My heart was pumping with excitement; not sure if it was because of the mission or because Paul and I were chatting.

After another hour or so, it was quiet. I figured one more hour of calmness and they all would be asleep except for a few roaming around. But to our amazement there really weren't any roaming guards, only a few on the road coming in. I suppose they thought they were invincible. That was about to change, and this was definitely good for us.

I signaled for the road to take out the guards first and then start with the C-4. He nodded in agreement. We crept up to the two men chatting sitting on rocks on the road. They were dead before they even stood up. Easy kill I would say, never even heard us coming.

Next Paul went to the left and I to the right. After I was done with the C-4, I made it back to the road with the two dead guys and waited for Paul to return. Wasn't too much longer and he showed up. We coordinated our

MONSTER

remote detonators to each building so I could have his and he had mine. We were in sync.

The plan was easy: we were going to enter each building and kill everyone inside with our pistols. They were the most silent of the two weapons. Even though we were shooting subsonic ammo, the rifle still was a bit louder.

I looked at him in good luck and shook his hand again. He looked at me and smiled and shook my hand. It was like we both knew we were going to die or something that night. It gave me an earie feeling, but then madness came over me and my game face was on. I was ready for battle.

The plan was that when we were done with each building, we would wait for the other one to come out before we proceeded. This way we had backup if needed. Should be an easy job for both of us. I was really hoping there weren't too many in each building; that always makes it a little more difficult, especially if you have a weapons failure.

I went into the first building, and only four people were in there, sound asleep. Took them out quickly and moved around to make sure no one else was there. All clear, and I went back out to wait for Paul.

I saw Paul come out and give me the OK. I gave him the OK back, and to the next building we proceeded. I went in and slaughtered all six in this one. Not even one woke up. I was hoping Paul had an easy one as well. I proceeded outside to wait for him, and he was already there with the OK. I gave it back to him and went to the next.

I walked in, but before I could even take a shot at the four that were in there, I heard gunfire. I quickly shot the four and ran outside to see one man by the door shooting an automatic gun into the building. I thought, Holy shit, this is bad! We were not even close to being done. What the hell happened? I quickly pulled up my rifle and shot him. I waited for Paul to come out, and nothing.

By this time, I could see and hear movement. It was time to blow the shit out of everything. I grabbed my remote and started in on the remaining building and left Paul's building alone just in case he was only wounded and not dead. The explosions were immense, to say the least. Shit was flying everywhere, and people were running naked and half-dressed in the middle. I stood there and shot them all, but a few took cover.

I kept looking for Paul, and nothing. Now I was even madder. I knew he was dead; I could feel it. I moved around some of the blown houses and found a living person here and another there, which I killed. I saw the big honcho come out and shot him in the leg. He was not leaving nowhere. His pain was going to be bad if Paul was dead.

I finally figured that most of them were dead or scattered. It was hard to tell because of the light. Couldn't see a lot but the burning buildings. I knew also that this would surely make others come to investigate what was going on. I walked over to the fat man and grabbed him by the hair and made him limp to the partial gate in front of town. "It's time for you, my friend."

I took out some paracord and told him to give me his hand or I would kill him. He obliged without a fight. I tied his wrist and then threw the cord over the top of the gate and tied it to the bottom, pulling him to his feet and stretched out. I then grabbed his other wrist and tied it and threw the paracord at the other end to spread him out even farther. Then I tied that to the bottom.

I then did the same to both ankles so he was a spread-eagle and begging for his life. I had no mercy because of Paul. I hope he was watching, if he was dead. Because this man was going to be quite the display.

I then went over to him and opened his shirt and cut it off of him and did the same with his pants so that he was naked. Then I cut his legs and arms wide open to the bone. Next I stuck my knife into his gut and slid the knife down to his penis and watched his guts fall out. The screaming was over with. I then took my pistol and shot the back of his neck, to break the bones in the spine so I could easily cut through them.

I took my knife and severed his head from his body. After that I found something to stand on and placed the head about a foot and a half above his body and tied it to the gate for all to see. I had a nice piece of paracord going through his mouth tied to the back of the gate. Then I tied another one to his forehead and secured the head. I didn't want it to fall.

Now it was time to go and find Paul and get the hell out of there. I went into the building to find several men and women dead in bed and Paul lying on the floor. He was dead with one good shot in the neck. My heart was broken. I know I didn't even know him, but we'd had a strong connection, and I was very upset about this. If this was to ever happen, we were supposed to dispose of the body, whether by blowing it up or burning it. I just couldn't do it. He needed to be brought back to his family, and they were going to do just that, or I was planning on killing them too. I was pissed.

I picked him up in a fireman's carry and put my rifle in hand. I knew now I couldn't drive out. Too many could be coming. I had to go back the same damn way I came in. This was going to be tough carrying him, but it needed to be done.

I packed him to rally point four and proceeded on. I needed to get out of there. Not sure if anyone would follow, considering the hideous scene I'd left them. I rather doubted it. I thought they would all be too scared to follow. I would have been if I had come upon a similar scene. I would definitely think it was the work of an army of crazies.

After a few hours of walking, I had to sit Paul down and get some water. I was really exhausted from carrying him, but I didn't care. He had to go back to his family.

After a short while, I could hear some noise. I knew someone was in the village; just hoped they stayed there or left. If they came after me, I was going to kill them even worse. My adrenaline was in high gear. I was ready for another battle. I was just so mad over Paul, my friend. We could have had some good conversations, but fuck no—he had to die for these fucking pigs. I felt like going back and killing anyone that showed up. Just mad!

MONSTER

I carried him as long as I could that day until the exhaustion took over. I lay down looking at him and just thinking. It was like he knew he was going to die. I don't know; it was just very strange to me. We'd had such a good time just messing with each other and being naughty by telling each other about our lives. We both knew that was a no-no, but for some strange reason we didn't care. I suppose we were more alike than we knew. I hoped one day in the future I'd find another monster that would chat with me.

I woke up the next day and picked Paul up and carried him to point one. By now I was fully exhausted, but I was almost on the road and could push the button for pickup. You probably wonder, but yes, I told Paul all about me on the hike back. I blabbed on for hours. Didn't even really care if anyone heard me. A few times I thought I heard him laugh. I kept telling him how he stank and was getting the last laugh by me carrying out his shitty stinking body. He must have laughed if he heard that.

I finally made it to the road and waited for the pickup. When the driver saw me come out with Paul's body, he was really shocked. He told me that he couldn't take him with us. I pulled out my pistol and said, "I hope you rethink what you just said." I think he could tell I wasn't in the mood for playing. Paul was going back to his family for a proper burial. And that was that.

I took a blanket and covered him up, and we went back to the safe house. I saw the driver go ahead of me. I was sure he was going to tell them about Paul. I didn't really give a shit. Our liaison came out and looked into the back of the truck and said, "We'll take care of him."

I looked hard at him and said, "What do you mean by that?"

He said, "We will make sure he gets back to his home and has a nice burial."

I told him, "I will be waiting to see. If not, I will come and find you again."

He just looked at me and asked, "How will you know if we do or not?"

I said, "I hope he has a nice funeral. If not, might be another one very soon."

He just looked at me and stated, "He will. I promise you that; I will make sure of it myself. If you like, you can escort the coffin on the plane."

I told him I would like that.

After all was said and done, I felt like Paul was given back to his family, so the liaison lived to see another day. Not sure what the government thought about it, but again I really didn't care at this point. It was the right thing to do. I just wished someday I could go and visit his children and tell them the truth maybe.

I would just tell them about how their dad was a member of an elite force protecting America. He gave his life saving mine. He was truly an American hero and should always be remembered as that, not a salesman. Good night, Paul. May God be with you always.

Chapter 16

BRUTALITY: LAST MISSION

Not a good way to start a mission. This mission was my worst one yet and my very last. It appeared that I'd gone too far on this one, and my mind was gone. I completely loss control of thinking correctly or logically. I was enraged, and brutality was up front and personal. I was no longer their guy but a brutal mass murderer. I would hope that one day this mission would leave my mind forever, but years later it is still there as though it was yesterday. God will not forgive me for what I did. I can't even come close to forgiving myself. I am a lost soul and forever in Lucifer's heart. I truly hate what I have become. No coming back from this; not even time or faith can help.

It was like any other mission; I would get a call and a place to meet. They would meet me and give me a debriefing of what to expect and what to do. As on any other mission, my whole purpose was to just kill and leave no one alive and whether it was drugs, money, or weapons, to leave all intact and push the button when the mission was done and leave. I assumed they came in and took the rest with no witnesses. I was the monster that did the dirty work, yet I did enjoy it. Yes, I said that. I thought I was doing it for my country and taking out the trash. But maybe I was helping the trash get rid of the trash. I will never know the meaning behind my work. I was a paid assassin, and I was an expert in my field. No conscience, no remorse, no feelings, no pain—nothing but a coldblooded killer. What a life I have lived and what a memory I must continue to live until the day I meet my new boss in hell. This is the last mission story.

I was sent down to South America to wipe out a large drug farm with expected personnel around thirty and well armed. Normally, for this size of operation, they would send one or two people to help me. For some reason it was just me. They loaded me up with Chinese weapons and clothing from a different country's military. They always did this so if I did die, there would be no trace back to the USA. I was invisible. I had no papers, no nothing that could trace me back. In anyone's eyes, it looked like I was being hired by someone else as a freelancer. It really didn't make me feel good about the setup, but my train of thought was, I don't care. I just wanted the excitement and adrenaline rush.

Oh, one thing that I've mentioned before that is important: they always stuck me with drugs. Again, I am not sure what was in them, but they made me feel mean and invincible. I think back and remember they were always telling me it was to protect me from disease and contamination in the area. Yeah, right. I know it was some mind-altering shit. My mind was clear as could ever be, and my temperament went through the roof. I was continually pissed off and wanted to kill everything in sight. That is not some kind of disease control. That was them making sure I completed the mission. Anyway, I will never know what they gave me. But I felt stronger and more powerful than anything ever. I never got sick; nothing ever happened to me. It truly was amazing the way I felt in a mission. Whether it was the adrenaline or drugs I have no idea.

On my last mission, I had the grid coordinates and all my accessories that I normally carried. That included my two syringes, one filled with lighter fluid for torture and one filled with household chemicals to inject into people and burn them from the inside out. I also carried a heavy-duty big-ass knife, spotting scope, and matches. The rest they issued to me: night vision googles, silencers, rifle, pistols, lots of ammo, Woobie, poncho, camo, GPS, compass, and map. Oh yes, the button for when everything was done.

I was put off about ten miles from the point of interest, and like I said, I was told to leave no witness alive; everyone must die. I got it. It was always that way. I shot my azimuth, and out I went. Normally in these types of missions, they would give me a heads-up and show me satellite photos of the area and the huts or buildings. This way I could see what I was up against and make my best way forward. They did that for this mission too. They seemed to have everything in place like any other deal. I was well informed of the circumstances and what waited for me. With the weapons I had, this would be easy with silencers and subsonic ammo. I could take most of them out without anyone even knowing I was there. Only downside was I was alone in this mission and didn't have additional help. It would have been nice to see another monster with me. But on the other hand, you never knew if they were to help you or kill you in the end. I figured that when meeting one of these vicious bastards, one of them would eventually kill me or I would be asked to kill them. One day I knew this was coming. I feel this was why some of the operators went rogue: because they had tried to take them out and failed. At least that was always in my head anyway.

As always, I had time on my side. My MO (mode of operation) was to get to an advantage point and observe for a day or two. Learn their habits, see how many came in and left on a daily basis. This was vital to an attack. It was great to know what their activities were.

I sat about four hundred meters away on a small hill, dug myself in, and made a little hole for me to hide in for a while. I watched downhill and tracked all their movements and made notes in my book. I could see lots of people down there who were not militants, just normal people working and packing. I assumed drugs. I saw one fat ass who looked like he was in charge wearing a sidearm on his hip and barking at people. He must have been the kingpin. At least now I knew who must die first. Take out the head honcho and most of the rest will most likely scatter. If they only knew what was about to happen, they would scatter now and get the fuck out of Dodge.

As I was watching fat ass, I saw him throughout the day going into one shack repeatably. I assumed this was his castle. He would be my first attack and little did I know my most brutal one. However, as I kept watching, I really didn't see much movement coming in and going out. Just a normal day of people walking around and security watching over a big shed. I had seen around six guards around a big shed. This must have been where the drugs were. Oh well, I didn't care about any of that. I also saw about four kids. Now this I didn't like at all. I was not a killer of children, and they *fucking* knew it. Why in the fuck would they put me in this situation? Unless they didn't know, but how could they not have known? They knew everything, and they knew I had a major issue with this.

I could not take my eyes off the children. I saw they were all young boys. No girls. Maybe the boys were being trained, or they were fat ass's children. I had no idea, but I was truly not a happy one. This caused a problem for me. I could see several women in the yard doing odd jobs like washing clothing and taking care of small tasks. I saw several guards that surrounded the perimeter. I only observed about four vehicles, though. I would have expected more, but four was enough, I supposed. One of my concerns was what I couldn't see. With this type of operation, there were sensors. I could see the guards were all staying in their areas and not moving outside of the area very much. This bothered me. I had to make sure and not give myself away, so I had to proceed carefully.

Nighttime was coming fast, and now I would get to see what was happening at night. This would be great intel. I sat in my spot and kept observing different things when something caught my eye. I saw the doors on the big shop open, and several more men and women came out. This really sucked. I'd thought I was looking at twenty-one, but now it was more like thirty-five. This was a shitload of people. I wondered, Where are they all going and sleeping, or are they leaving and coming back? What the hell is going on now? What are they doing in there?

I was kind of hoping they would all leave but really didn't see anyone leaving; they were out eating and drinking. Which struck me weird. The women were all together mostly, and men were in their little cliques. Then one or two would grab a woman and take her to the hacienda. Not sure if this was a willing interaction with a girlfriend or rape. Of course, I was not there to wonder; I was there to observe their actions and find the best place to attack and kill. Like I said, I was well armed and had a vest on. I had to take out the guards first and foremost and then deal with the leftovers. I wasn't much afraid of this; these were not well-trained military, just some low-life druggies.

A well-trained force would have not left his post to go pee and leave it open, nor would he leave and keep looking away from it. They were just men with guns. Nothing more. This job is easy, I thought. This is why I am by myself. Shouldn't be difficult at all.

MONSTER

Throughout the night I kept an eye on all of them and saw when they went to bed and how long they stood up. I made detailed notes on all of them. I made names for each of them and wrote down what they did. Like fat ass: He lived in this one place with a cow horn on the side. He was at the end of the area. I guess he needed his solitude from the other peasants. Which was good for me; no one would see me go into his hut first. Don't get me wrong: he wasn't that far from the others, just a little way away.

I made notes of each guard and where they slept and who relieved them. I also noticed a small four-man roving patrol. These guys did nothing but yack the entire time. They must have felt like nothing would ever happen to them. They were not on guard, just had to do this minimal task. That was great for me, and they would be easy to take out.

I finally didn't see much movement, so I grabbed a little shut-eye and waited for morning to see what was going on then. After about 6:00 a.m., I saw some movement and but was also happy to see some of the guards napping. It seemed so sloppy, but sloppy was good from my perspective. These were not well trained at all for this kind of operation. I assumed lots of drugs were coming in from somewhere and leaving to somewhere. But so far, no vehicles had left. This did strike me as weird. I would have thought people would have been coming and leaving. But nothing. OK. Then I saw some of the women being talked to by guards and apparently being told to go cook. OK, that was normal. Nothing had gone into the building yet. I wondered if there was more in the building that I had not seen. Surely they had guards inside, but how many? I would have had some in there. But I had not seen anyone yet. So maybe not. After the next hour or so, I saw most of the people change out, eat, and do other normal activities.

Then I finally saw a truck come up. It had only two occupants in there. They drove over to the fat ass's house and waited. He then strolled out like King Tut. I really couldn't wait to kill him. They looked like they were chatting for a while, and then they got back into the vehicle and left. They didn't take anything or leave anything. That I thought was strange. But the less the merrier.

I had a good idea of how things were going to go tonight. There was really no need to wait any more. Tonight, I would attack the roving guards on both sides and then make my way to each guard and then go to fat ass's house. After that I had two main houses where I needed to kill the rest of the men and then the women. I still had very mixed emotions about the boys. But I did see one of them with fat ass, so they must have been his kids, and that was good enough, I guessed. We don't want to carry on that gene pool, I thought. Maybe they knew I would see this and figure that out. These children were his and needed to die as well. I guess that gave me some comfort. Not much, but some.

Time passed slowly that day. I saw people walking around doing their thing, while others were put into the shed to do whatever they were doing in there. I really didn't care. At this point I was getting mad and wanted to go get into the shit, start the mission, finish it, and go home. I really felt like this was just going to be like any other in and out. I figured thirty-one minutes tops and they all would be dead. I calculated the time it would take me to move from house to house and how many were in each and knew they would only take seconds to kill. Easy peasy.

Nighttime came, and it was time for me to move. I could see all of them eating and drinking the same as before. I had to get into place for the shift change and take out the roving guards first. I decided to go behind the fat ass's house and kill those guards first because of distances, and then when the other guards who were around fifteen minutes away came, I would kill them. Tuck them all away in a cubby hole and then the rest. All great plans. But fuck no! Nothing ever goes as planned.

I finally made it back with any trip flares or sensors. I'd seen nothing, which I thought unusual. But hey, let's go for it, I told myself. I saw two of the roving guards coming down the path behind fat ass's house. So I just waited in the trees about twenty feet away from the path. They were going to get a bullet in the head, and then I'd drag them back to where I was and wait for the next ones to come around.

The two made their way to me, chatting up a storm. When they passed me, I put my gun on them and shot them both dead in a split second. They were dead before they even hit the ground. Nicely done, I thought. I hurried up and dragged them out of the way. So far so good.

I saw fat ass coming to his house with his son. No big deal. I didn't pay much mind to it really. I was close to his one-room little shack. I could hear some arguing inside. No big deal. Father's son deal. But the sounds from the kid were muffled like Dad was putting his hands over his mouth. I did find that strange and thought, What the hell is that about?

I guess curiosity got the best of me, and I knew I had about ten minutes before the other patrol made it to me. So what the hell, I thought. Let me see what is going on in there. My heart is killing me right now writing this. Very bad memories are coming forward, and I can feel my blood pressure rising…I saw that the fat-ass son of a bitch had the boy's hands tied together in the back. Tape was over his mouth and he was naked bent over the bed while the fat son of a bitch was fucking him. This is where I loss control and shit went crazy for me.

I went into the house and grabbed the man's mouth from behind and stuck my knife up his bare ass as he screamed into my palm. I then took my knife and cut him down the spinal cord to his ass on both sides. Then I proceeded to stab him repeatedly in the back. After he was good and dead, I pulled him off the kid and sat the boy in the corner. I then went back and took fat ass's head almost completely off; I cut his chest open and slit him down to his penis. I took his penis off with his balls and stuffed them in his mouth. I cut him into pieces. I stabbed him in the chest twenty times while the kids just sat there crying. I must have looked like a complete monster. In fact, I was a monster now.

After I hacked his body into pieces, I must have looked like a bloody fucking mess. I was filled with kill and rage. I was crazy mad. I can't even explain the rage. I wasn't just going to kill everyone; I was going to massacre them.

I forgot about the boy until I looked up and saw his eyes. I went over to him and sat down for a moment. I put my fingers to my mouth to keep him quiet. He was crying and scared. I was even getting madder than before for what they have done to him. I am sure they were all just sex toys.

I asked the boy, "Puedes estar callado?" (Can you be quiet?) He shook his head yes. "Lo siento," I said. (I'm sorry for this.) "Si te dejo ir, te irás y no se lo dirás a nadie?" (If I let you go, will you leave and not tell anyone?)

He was crying and shook his head yes. I went back to fat ass's pants and went through them and found lots of money. I also found lots in his small desk. I gathered it up and put it in the boy's clothes. I told him, "This is for you and your family. You must follow me, and I will lead you out of here." He nodded his head. I untied him and told him to get dressed. He did as I asked and had pockets full of money. I led him out the back and took him to the field and told him to run and not ever come back. He looked at me and hugged me and then took off.

After I saw him leave and he was out of sight, the rage came back in full force. I no longer cared about doing things right. I went back in the fat ass's house and let the black monster come out. I just walked out and started in. I went from house to house and killed everything. I killed and cut up women and men left and right. I heard screaming and gunfire. I stepped out like nothing and killed them with no fear for my own life. I couldn't believe what they were doing to children. I had no idea why they didn't hit me with any rounds, but they were dropping like flies. I just walked around and killed everything that moved. I even took time to cut heads off with a machete I found. I stood over one man and cut him into four pieces. I just didn't care about dying at this point. One woman ran over to me as if to ask for help. I took her whole head off with the machete.

I had no remorse for anything; I was out to kill them all and mutilate their bodies. I saw some of the young boys running. I let them go but no one else. I vowed I would track them down and kill them with vengeance. No one was leaving this place alive. They wanted to be monsters; let them meet one. I shot and killed most of them, and the rest I killed with the machete. Then after everyone seemed to be dead, I did the most horrific thing possible. I went looking for anyone else alive and when I found a body, I mutilated it. I cut open the guts, took off the heads, cut the heads in half, took off feet, and went crazy. This scene was a total nightmare. I can only imagine what people thought when they came here. It was not just a killing but a fucking horror story times ten.

I can remember throwing body parts at the shop, hoping someone would come out. Screaming like a mad man. No one was safe. They died ten times after death. I could not stop hacking bodies up. I was insane.

I wanted to leave a message for people like this. That a monster came and did the unthinkable and that is what I did. Probably no one had ever witnessed this kind of brutality, and no one would have believed it was from one person. I'm not sure if it was the drugs I was given or seeing the boy being raped. But whatever kicked in was wicked and ugly.

I walked over to the shed and opened it like I owned it. Guess what? A bunch of drugs and money and weapons. What a fucking shocker! I think this made me even more enraged. I really wanted to burn it to the ground. I didn't; I just walked back to fat ass's house, took his fucking head with dick and balls in his mouth, and sat it on top of the drugs. I went back out to make more of statement after that. I continued to chop off limbs and heads and throw them all over the place. This place was one for even hell to look at. Lucifer must have been proud of me that day.

I sat down and had the thousand-yard stare at what I had done. (The thousand-yard stare is when a soldier has seen too much and has no emotions.) I knew I'd gone too far, but I couldn't let children be hurt for some scum's sexual pleasure.

After I was finally done and calmed down, I pushed the button and laughed and said, "Come get some of this, you fucking bastards."

I left the bloody scene and went back through the jungle to get back to the hotel. After a little while, I made it to my pack, which had extra clothes to change into. By this time, I could see myself, and I looked like the true monster that I am. There is no coming back from this, I told myself. You really fucked this one up.

I don't know why I committed these atrocities. Why I went so far. I guess all the years of killing finally pushed me over the edge, and I was no longer sane. I was an animal—a monster—that should be put to death. What life could I have after this? I was evil!

I cleaned myself up and walked back to the hotel with my weapons and monster clothes in my bag and sat there wondering what I had done. Wasn't long before I was picked up in silence and taken to the airport and I left.

The mission was over, and they surely had seen what I had done. I would have thought they would have killed me after that or done something with me. But it wasn't long before I realized that I was no use to them anymore, and I was dismissed into the shadows and never talked to them again. I got nothing from them but my usual bonus and paycheck and was never asked to do anything ever again. I guess they retired me and left me the way I was. Maybe they realized that I had no further use because I was out of control. I did leave a head for them on top of the drugs. Maybe that was a signal that I was tired of this. Maybe it was because I let kids live. Maybe it was because my mind had snapped. I will never know what happened to me or why, but I do know that coping with it has been very difficult.

As I stated earlier, you never know when you will come across a monster, but pray you never do. They are pure evil with no thoughts of killing, and they have no rules. They are protected and very secretly hidden in the walls.

Chapter 17

LIVING WITH YOURSELF

I went back to my normal life and waited for the worst. I had no idea what was coming after that ordeal. I know I went too far on that mission. I really don't know if it was the drugs they were giving me or if it was just the child in danger. All I know is I lost my mind on that mission and there is never a chance of erasing that or ever forgetting what I did. I was a complete monster and ruthless killer.

I know if I had gone on any more missions, they probably would have been worse than that one. I have no remorse or conscience anymore; I am just a monster and loved the kill. They got what they wanted. I was theirs entirely.

For some strange reason, they never called me back, and my career was over. I guess they figured I had lost my mind completely. I really thought they would send someone out to kill me, but they never did. Maybe I was an experiment, and they wanted to see if I could adjust back into normal, everyday life after something like that. Still to this day, no one has ever contacted me. In fact, my oil field career died along with that day. I was becoming less important to the oil field and nonimportant to them.

After a few years of demoting and moving me, the oil field let me go. Even though I was still young and they had no apparent reason, they just one day let me go and blamed it on the COVID-19 pandemic. How convenient was that timing? Which was OK. I needed to retire and just live a simple life alone and die off into the abyss.

I never even thought about writing a book about my life, mostly because I was afraid of retaliation, but the closer you get to death, the scariness just doesn't seem to matter anymore. I was over them, and they were over me. I was OK with that, I guess.

I am going to publish this as a fictional book, though. You can surely believe what I've written down here or not. I really don't care at all. Like I said, many times individual people are smart, but a group of people are nothing more than sheep. They believe everything the government says. They tell you they are helping you; in reality they are only helping themselves.

Let me give you an example of how they brainwash you. Remember the COVID pandemic? They had everyone in a panic, buying up everything and thinking they were going to die. Don't get me wrong; people did die, just not as many as you think. For example, people die every year from the flu. But when the pandemic came around, they all died of COVID. Remarkable how no one died of the flu during that time, isn't it?

Look at it this way too. The hospitals were getting government money for any COVID-related death. Can you really imagine that? You could tie anything to COVID. So they did. This also made the public cower in fear. Lo and behold, the government came out and saved you all. They found a cure for all. Yeah, that didn't turn out worth a shit. People were still getting COVID. Remember that the FDA takes years to accept a cure because they need to do long-term and short-term studies. Did you see any long-term studies, or did you just see the two-month version?

When you took the drug, did it save you from getting COVID? No, of course not; it was not a cure at all. In fact, the government came out with another concept: "You will not have COVID as rough because the vaccine will help you." Yeah, that was a lie too. Make no mistake: lots of people in the government made millions off this, and you thanked them. This is the brainwashing I am talking about. They tell you how to think, and you end up thanking them.

I never took the COVID shot and have never been sick in twenty-plus years. Like I said, I do know the cure for flu and cancer. It's right there, but you all are too blind to see. I would in fact love to help some of you through it. But on the other hand, I ask, why bother? I am not here to convince you of anything, just to inform you that the government is very well versed in brainwashing. As I described earlier in this book, at one point I was literally thanking them for an Oreo when in fact they were breaking me down. I just had to think they were helping me. Isn't that ironic?

I had no clue what they were doing to me at the time. I thought they were actually great people helping me. But when the light went on and I saw reality, I was shocked. It's OK; they are good at what they do. I just hope someday other people wake up instead of being sheep led to the slaughterhouse.

I want to reiterate that I love my country and really thought I was doing their work, but after years of doing horrible things and slaughtering people for guns, money, and drugs to fund other areas, it took a toll on my head. I understand why they made me do the things they made me do. I get it. They have to have so-called money to operate in other areas, as well as drugs and guns you can sell to anyone, even your enemies, if you have a bigger picture. I get that. I also am not sorry for my life and what I have done. I really did enjoy most of the missions. I guess the last mission is when everything came into reality for me. I then realized after seeing what I did that I had become the monster, what I hated the most.

I struggle every day seeing the children on the news being hurt by these people. Every day I wish to cause them great harm. But there is only me, and if I was ever caught killing these people, would I be praised in America or lethally injected? Not hard to know that answer. I would be put to death for these sick individuals that keep getting away time and time again.

I really hope one day Americans can wake up and take action because we are tired of our children and neighbors being hurt by the wicked people that roam our streets. I personally feel that our humanity has failed in life. There are no good people left in this world. I am not good either. I have done horrific things in the name of this country and still think about doing them again today.

It's a complete struggle for someone like me who has seen and caused so many deaths. The only innocent ones are our children, and even some of those are not. How can we change? I don't know; maybe a nuclear war is the answer. Maybe we need to start from scratch again and try over like so many civilizations before us. I think we are at our end.

Until the end comes, though, I know there will always be people like me. The American people need them. I was only a small part of the organization. Who knows how many other areas there are? I only knew my job. I had never even heard of someone like me before I was recruited. Didn't even know they existed. That is how in the dark we are.

I have lots of regrets; I can say that. Some of me wishes I lived just a normal life and didn't see what I have seen. I wish I was just a sheep and walked around with my eyes closed. That is the life I sometimes wish I could have lived. But there is the other part that really enjoyed saving some kid in the jungle too.

I also wish that if I ever do publish this book and there is someone out there like me who wants to chat, he will be willing to meet me. I would love to know how they cope with life after seeing and doing what we did.

I am grateful that I don't get sick and nothing is ever wrong with me. Whatever they gave me, I am grateful for it. I have felt like superman for most of my life. The government truly has some great drugs, which is why some never die except in old age. I find that amazing; they never have cancer or are sick unless they are not liked.

I often thought I was going to die in combat but never did. And now I am existing in life with horrible people every day. I am not sure how to handle it sometimes. But I do know there are three ways out.

The first way out is just dying in combat or whatever. I thought for years they were going to kill me off. That never happened. I also thought on a few missions that the other person like me was going to kill me after the mission, but that never happened. Plus, he probably thought the same thing about me.

Second, finding good women is another way out. It's hard to feel whole without a partner in life. We are not meant to go through life alone. If you find that one soul mate, then you have hit the lottery. That can pull you from the depths of hell.

Third, God. In my earlier life, I had found God, and then I lost him again. Now I read the Bible and talk to as many people as I can about him. However, there is a part of me that feels forgotten. I don't feel the love anymore from him. I guess I deserve that. I have been a monster for so long that there can't be any coming back. That is OK; I have accepted it in my heart. But after the monster incident during my last mission, I vowed to be a good man until I die and to do the best I can in this life. I have promised myself to God and will live the remaining years by his word. I hope that one day he can forgive someone like me. If not, when I go to hell, I will still stand by God and fight the devil for eternity. I am your loving son, God, and I am truly sorry for my actions in this life.

I know this book is hard for most people to truly comprehend, and I accept that. I don't even believe the things I did, but I did them. I hope you people understand that the government in their own way does try and protect us. Not always, but not all of them are after money and filling their pockets. Some are actually after our safety.

We cannot really control the government, but we can control our lives. Only our lives. We can't control other people and their wicked ways. If you find these types of people, stay away from them; don't let them control your emotions. There are those people that have no good in them. They are miserable from the core; these people need to be alone and never let into your life. They are the truly evil people in this world. They might not hurt you physically, but mentally they will destroy you. This is what I refer to when I talk about the wickedness of humanity.

I want to tell you I am not just preaching to you about wicked people; I am one. However, going forward I am trying to see the good in people, but someone like me sees the bad very quickly. I see the user for what they are. I see those who try and control others emotionally for who they are. But remember, seeing all the inhuman things in people can really sometimes bring out the godliness in others.

Do not let anyone treat you badly; stay away from them. Treat people well, and maybe one day you can change your behavior and have humanity back in your life. I do believe that you can't ever treat some people well. They should just die so we are rid of them. Yes, I said that. Some you can't change, and some will never change. This is life as we know it.

Two more pieces of advice. Watch the news daily, and see how they control your mind. They tell you what to think and only show you the horrific things in life: war, shootings, etc. Just turn it off and live your life the best you can; don't be brainwashed by the news or the government. This is your only life. Live it and love it.

Next, as I mentioned earlier in the book, I hope you people never come across those like me. If you do, please be nice to all that you meet. They are truly monsters and are capable of horrific things. These are not the kinds of people you wish to make your enemy; they are patient and planning but ruthless, wicked individuals.

What you do with this book is up to you. Whether you believe the material or not is up to you. But know this: we are out there, and we truly believe we are protecting you. We are not out there killing the good people, only those that deserve to be gotten rid of. Yes, maybe some of us enjoyed our job too much, but in the back of our minds we believed we were your sheepdog protecting *you*.

Let me finish up with a warning. Even though I'm trying to live a good life, there are still times when it's tough not to become what I once was. People are horrible and constantly push my patience; they have no idea what thoughts go through my head and how close they sometimes come to the ends of their lives. Be careful around those you treat with disrespect; they might be the last person you ever see.

A person like me expects to die in battle, not grow old and die of old age, You could be his way out of normalcy. Let me put it another way: be kind to those you meet; you never know their monsters that lie within.

P.S. Here's a final thought for you. Ever wonder why you wake up sometimes at 3:00 a.m.? I know, and so does the government. We never attack at that time because lots of people wake up then; instead we come early. Sleep well, my friends.